Robert Bloch (1917-1994) was a prolific American writer, primarily of crime, horror, fantasy and science fiction. He is best known as the writer of *Psycho*, the basis for the film of the same name by Alfred Hitchcock. He wrote 'Despite my ghoulish reputation, I really have the heart of a small boy. I keep it in a jar on my desk.' — a quote borrowed by Stephen King and often misattributed to him. Bloch wrote hundreds of short stories and over 30 novels, and was one of the youngest members of the Lovecraft Circle. A contributor to pulp magazines such as *Weird Tales* in his early career, a prolific screenwriter and a major contributor to science fiction fanzines and fandom in general, his accolades included the Hugo Award, the Bram Stoker Award, and the World Fantasy Award. His work has been extensively filmed for cinema and television.

PSYCHO

She was a fugitive, lost in a storm. That was when she saw the sign: MOTEL — VACANCY. She switched off the engine and sat thinking, alone and frightened. The stolen money wouldn't help her, and Sam couldn't either, because she had taken the wrong turning. There was nothing she could do now — she had made her grave and she'd have to lie in it . . . She froze. Where had *that* come from? It was *bed*, not *grave*. She shivered in the cold car, surrounded by shadows. Then, without a sound, a dark shape emerged from the blackness and the car door opened . . .

ROBERT BLOCH

PSYCHO

Complete and Unabridged

ULVERSCROFT
Leicester

First published in Great Britain in 1959

First Large Print Edition
published 2014
by arrangement with
Robert Hale Limited
London

Copyright © 1959 by Robert Bloch

C460344987

A catalogue record for this book is available
from the British Library.

ISBN 978-1-4448-1854-3

Published by
F. A. Thorpe (Publishing)
Anstey, Leicestershire

Set by Words & Graphics Ltd.
Anstey, Leicestershire
Printed and bound in Great Britain by
T. J. International Ltd., Padstow, Cornwall

This book is printed on acid-free paper

10%
of this book
is dedicated to
Harry Altshuler,
who did 90% of the work

1

Norman Bates heard the noise and a shock went through him.

It sounded as though somebody was tapping on the windowpane.

He looked up, hastily, half prepared to rise, and the book slid from his hands to his ample lap. Then he realized that the sound was merely rain. Late afternoon rain, striking the parlor window.

Norman hadn't noticed the coming of the rain, nor the twilight. But it was quite dim here in the parlor now, and he reached over to switch on the lamp before resuming his reading.

It was one of those old-fashioned table lamps, the kind with the ornate glass shade and the crystal fringe. Mother had had it ever since he could remember, and she refused to get rid of it. Norman didn't really object; he had lived in this house for all of the forty years of his life, and there was something quite pleasant and reassuring about being surrounded by familiar things. Here everything was orderly and ordained; it was only there, outside, that the changes took place.

And most of those changes held a potential threat. Suppose he had spent the afternoon walking, for example? He might have been off on some lonely side road or even back in the swamps when the rain came, and then what? He'd be soaked to the skin, forced to stumble along home in the dark. You could catch your death of cold that way, and besides, who wanted to be out in the dark? It was much nicer here in the parlor, under the lamp, with a good book for company.

The light shone down on his plump face, reflected from his rimless glasses, bathed the pinkness of his scalp beneath the thinning sandy hair as he bent his head to resume reading.

It was really a fascinating book — no wonder he hadn't noticed how fast the time had passed. It was *The Realm of the Incas*, by Victor W. Von Hagen, and Norman had never before encountered such a wealth of curious information. For example, this description of the *cachua*, or victory dance, where the warriors formed a great circle, moving and writhing like a snake. He read:

The drumbeat for this was usually performed on what had been the body of an enemy: the skin had been flayed and the belly stretched to form a drum, and the whole body acted as a sound box while throbbings came out of the open mouth — grotesque, but effective.[1]

Norman smiled, then allowed himself the luxury of a comfortable shiver. *Grotesque but effective* — it certainly *must* have been! Imagine flaying a man — alive, probably — and then stretching his belly to use it as a drum! How did they actually go about doing that, curing and preserving the flesh of the corpse to prevent decay? For that matter, what kind of a mentality did it take to conceive of such an idea in the first place?

It wasn't the most appetizing notion in the world, but when Norman half closed his eyes, he could almost see the scene: this throng of painted, naked warriors wriggling and swaying in unison under a sun-drenched, savage sky, and the old crone crouching before them, throbbing out a relentless rhythm on the swollen, distended belly of a cadaver. The contorted mouth of the corpse would be forced open, probably fixed in a gaping grimace by clamps of bone, and from it the sound emerged. Beating from the belly, rising through the shrunken inner orifices, forced up through the withered windpipe to emerge

---

[1] Reprinted by permission of the author.

amplified and in full force from the dead throat.

For a moment, Norman could almost hear it, and then he remembered that rain has its rhythm too, and footsteps —

Actually, he was aware of the footsteps without even hearing them; long familiarity aided his senses whenever Mother came into the room. He didn't even have to look up to know she was there.

In fact, he *didn't* look up; he pretended to continue his reading, instead. Mother had been sleeping in her room, and he knew how crabby she could get when just awakened. So it was best to keep quiet and hope that she wasn't in one of her bad moods.

'Norman, do you know what time it is?'

He sighed and closed the book. He could tell now that she was going to be difficult; the very question was a challenge. Mother had to pass the grandfather clock in the hall in order to come in here and she could easily see what time it was.

Still, no sense making an issue of it. Norman glanced down at his wrist watch, then smiled. 'A little after five,' he said. 'I actually didn't realize it was so late. I've been reading — '

'Don't you think I have eyes? I can see what you've been doing.' She was over at the window now, staring out at the rain. 'And I can see what you haven't been doing, too. Why didn't you turn the sign on when it got dark? And why aren't you up at the office where you belong?'

'Well, it started to rain so hard, and I didn't expect there'd be any traffic in this kind of weather.'

'Nonsense! That's just the time you're likely to get some business. Lots of folks don't care to drive when it's raining.'

'But it isn't likely anybody would be coming this way. Everyone takes the new highway.' Norman heard the bitterness creeping into his voice, felt it welling up into his throat until he could taste it, and tried to hold it back. But too late now; he had to vomit it out. 'I told you how it would be at the time, when we got that advance tip that they were moving the highway. You could have sold the motel then, before there was a public announcement about the new road coming through. We could have bought all kinds of land over there for a song, closer to Fairvale, too. We'd have had a new motel, a new house, made some money. But you wouldn't listen. You never listen to me, do you? It's always what *you* want and what *you* think. You make me sick!'

'Do I, boy?' Mother's voice was deceptively

gentle, but that didn't fool Norman. Not when she called him 'boy.' Forty years old, and she called him 'boy': that's how she treated him, too, which made it worse. If only he didn't have to listen! But he did, he knew he had to, he always had to listen.

'Do I, boy?' she repeated, even more softly. 'I make you sick, eh? Well, I think not. No, boy, *I* don't make you sick. You make *yourself* sick.

'That's the real reason you're still sitting over here on this side road, isn't it, Norman? Because the truth is that you haven't any gumption. *Never* had any gumption, did you, boy?

'Never had the gumption to leave home. Never had the gumption to go out and get yourself a job, or join the army, or even find yourself a girl — '

'You wouldn't let me!'

'That's right, Norman. I wouldn't let you. But if you were half a man, you'd have gone your own way.'

He wanted to shout out at her that she was wrong, but he couldn't. Because the things she was saying were the things he had told himself, over and over again, all through the years. It was true. She'd always laid down the law to him, but that didn't mean he always had to obey. Mothers sometimes

6

are overly possessive, but not all children allow themselves to be possessed. There had been other widows, other only sons, and not all of them became enmeshed in this sort of relationship. It was really his fault as much as hers. Because he didn't have any gumption.

'You could have insisted, you know,' she was saying. 'Suppose you'd gone out and found us a new location, then put the place here up for sale. But no, all you did was whine. And I know why. You never fooled me for an instant. It's because you really didn't *want* to move. You've never wanted to leave this place, and you never will now, ever. You *can't* leave, can you? Any more than you can grow up.'

He couldn't look at her. Not when she said things like that, he couldn't. And there was nowhere else for him to look, either. The beaded lamp, the heavy old overstuffed furniture, all the familiar objects in the room, suddenly became hateful just *because* of long familiarity; like the furnishings of a prison cell. He stared out of the window, but that was no good either — out there was the wind and the rain and the darkness. He knew there was no escape for him out *there*. No escape anywhere, from the voice that throbbed, the voice that drummed into his ears like that of

7

the Inca corpse in the book; the drum of the dead.

He clutched at the book now and tried to focus his eyes on it. Maybe if he ignored her, and pretended to be calm —

But it didn't work.

'Look at yourself!' she was saying (*the drum going boom-boom-boom, and the sound reverberating from the mangled mouth*). 'I know why you didn't bother to switch on the sign. I know why you haven't even gone up to open the office tonight. You didn't really forget. It's just that you don't *want* anyone to come, you hope they *don't* come.'

'All right!' he muttered. 'I admit it. I hate running a motel, always have.'

'It's more than that, boy.' (*There it was again, 'Boy, boy, boy!' drumming away, out of the jaws of death.*) 'You hate *people*. Because, really, you're *afraid* of them, aren't you? Always have been, ever since you were a little tyke. Rather snuggle up in a chair under the lamp and read. You did it thirty years ago, and you're still doing it now. Hiding away under the covers of a book.'

'There's a lot worse things I could be doing. You always told me that, yourself. At least I never went out and got into trouble. Isn't it better to improve my mind?'

8

'Improve your mind? Hah!' He could sense her standing behind him now, staring down. 'Call *that* improvement? You don't fool me, boy, not for a minute. Never have. It isn't as if you were reading the Bible, or even trying to get an education. I know the sort of thing *you* read. Trash. And worse than trash!'

'This happens to be a history of the Inca civilization — '

'I'll just bet it is. And I'll just bet it's crammed full with nasty bits about those dirty savages, like the one you had about the South Seas. Oh, you didn't think I knew about *that* one, did you? Hiding it up in your room, the way you hid all the others, those filthy things you used to read — '

'Psychology isn't filthy, Mother!'

'Psychology, he calls it! A lot *you* know about psychology! I'll never forget that time you talked so dirty to me, never. To think that a son could come to his own mother and *say* such things!'

'But I was only trying to explain something. It's what they call the Oedipus situation, and I thought if both of us could just look at the problem reasonably and try to understand it, maybe things would change for the better.'

'Change, boy? Nothing's going to change. You can read all the books in the world and you'll still be the same. I don't need to listen to a lot of vile, obscene rigamarole to know what you are. Why, even a eight-year-old child could recognize it. They *did*, too, all your little playmates did, way back then. You're a Mamma's Boy. That's what they called you, and that's what you were. Were, are, and always will be. A big, fat, overgrown Mamma's Boy!'

It was deafening him, the drumbeat of her words, the drumbeat in his own chest. The vileness in his mouth made him choke. In a moment he'd have to cry. Norman shook his head. To think that she could still do this to him, even now! But she could, and she was, and she *would*, over and over again, unless —

'Unless what?'

God, could she read his *mind?*

'I know what you're thinking, Norman. I know all about you, boy. More than you dream. But I know that, too — what you dream. You're thinking that you'd like to kill me, aren't you, Norman? But you can't. Because you haven't the gumption. I'm the one who has the strength. I've always had it. Enough for both of us. That's why you'll never get rid of me, even if you really wanted to.

'Of course, deep down, you *don't* want to. You need me, boy. That's the truth, isn't it?'

Norman stood up, slowly. He didn't dare trust himself to turn and face her, not yet. He had to tell himself to be calm, first. Be very, very calm. Don't think about what she's saying. Try to face up to it, try to remember. *She's an old woman, and not quite right in the head. If you keep on listening to her this way, you'll end up not quite right in the head, either. Tell her to go back to her room and lie down. That's where she belongs.*

And she'd better go there fast, because if she doesn't, this time you're going to strangle her with her own Silver Cord —

He started to swing around, his mouth working, framing the phrases, when the buzzer sounded.

That was the signal; it meant somebody had driven in, up at the motel, and was ringing for service.

Without even bothering to look back, Norman walked into the hall, took his raincoat from the hanger, and went out into the darkness.

2

The rain had been falling steadily for several minutes before Mary noticed it and switched on the windshield wiper. At the same time she put on the headlights; it had gotten dark quite suddenly, and the road ahead was only a vague blur between the towering trees.

Trees? She couldn't recall a stretch of trees along here the last time she'd driven this way. Of course that had been the previous summer and she'd come into Fairvale in broad daylight, alert and refreshed. Now she was tired out from eighteen hours of steady driving, but she could still remember and sense that something was wrong.

Remember — that was the trigger word. Now she *could* remember, dimly, how she'd hesitated back there about a half-hour ago, when she came to the fork in the road. That was it; she'd taken the wrong turn. And now here she was, God knows where, with this rain coming down and everything pitch-black outside —

Get a grip on yourself, now. You can't afford to be panicky. The worst part of it is over.

It was true, she told herself. The worst part was over. The worst part had come yesterday afternoon, when she stole the money.

She had been standing in Mr. Lowery's office when old Tommy Cassidy hauled out that big green bundle of bills and put them down on the desk. Thirty-six Federal Reserve notes bearing the picture of the fat man who looked like a wholesale grocer, and eight more carrying the face of the man who looked like an undertaker. But the wholesale grocer was Grover Cleveland and the undertaker was William McKinley. And thirty-six thousands and eight five-hundreds added up to forty thousand dollars.

Tommy Cassidy had put them down just like *that*, fanning them casually as he announced he was closing the deal and buying a house as his daughter's wedding present.

Mr. Lowery pretended to be just as casual as he went through the business of signing the final papers. But after old Tommy Cassidy went away, Mr. Lowery got a little bit excited. He scooped up the money, put it into a big brown Manila number ten envelope, and sealed the flap. Mary noticed how his hands were trembling.

'Here,' he said, handing her the money. 'Take it over to the bank. It's almost four o'clock, but I'm sure Gilbert will let you make a deposit.' He paused, staring at her. 'What's the matter, Miss Crane — don't you feel well?'

Maybe he had noticed the way *her* hands trembled, now that she was holding the envelope. But it didn't matter. She knew what she was going to say, even though she was surprised when she found herself actually saying it.

'I seem to have one of my headaches, Mr. Lowery. As a matter of fact, I was just going to ask if it was all right if I took the rest of the afternoon off. We're all caught up on the mail, and we can't make out the rest of the forms on this deal until Monday.'

Mr. Lowery smiled at her. He was in good humor, and why shouldn't he be? Five per cent of forty thousand was two thousand dollars. He could afford to be generous.

'Of course, Miss Crane. You just make this deposit and then run along home. Would you like me to drive you?'

'No, that's all right, I can manage. A little rest — '

'That's the ticket. See you Monday, then. Take it easy, that's what I always say.'

In a pig's ear that's what *he* always said: Lowery would half kill himself to make an extra dollar, and he'd be perfectly willing to kill any of his employees for another fifty cents.

But Mary Crane had smiled at him very sweetly, then walked out of his office and out of his life. Taking the forty thousand dollars with her.

You don't get that kind of an opportunity every day of your life. In fact, when you come right down to it, some people don't seem to get *any* opportunities at all.

Mary Crane had waited over twenty-seven years for hers.

The opportunity to go on to college had vanished, at seventeen, when Daddy was hit by a car. Mary went to business school for a year, instead, and then settled down to support Mom and her kid sister, Lila.

The opportunity to marry disappeared at twenty-two, when Dale Belter was called up to serve his hitch in the army. Pretty soon he was stationed in Hawaii, and before long he began mentioning this girl in his letters, and then the letters stopped coming. When she finally got the wedding announcement she didn't care any more.

Besides, Mom was pretty sick by then. It took her three years to die, while Lila was off at school. Mary had insisted she get to college, come what may, but that left her carrying the whole load. Between holding down a job at the Lowery Agency all day and sitting up with Mom half the night, there wasn't time for anything else.

Not even time to note the *passing* of time. But then Mom had the final stroke, and there was the business of the funeral, and Lila coming back from school and trying to find a job, and all at once there was Mary Crane looking at herself in the big mirror and seeing this drawn, contorted face peering back at her. She'd thrown something at the mirror, and then the mirror broke into a thousand pieces and she knew that wasn't all; *she* was breaking into a thousand pieces, too.

Lila had been wonderful and even Mr. Lowery helped out by seeing to it that the house was sold right away. By the time the estate was settled they had about two thousand dollars in cash left over. Lila got a job in a record shop downtown, and they moved into a small apartment together.

'Now you're going to take a vacation,' Lila told her. 'A real vacation. No, don't argue about it! You've kept this family going for eight years and it's about time you had a rest. I want you to take a trip. A cruise, maybe.'

So Mary took the *S.S. Caledonia*, and after a week or so in Caribbean waters the drawn, contorted face had disappeared from the mirror of her stateroom. She looked like a

16

young girl again (well, certainly not a day over twenty-two, she told herself) and, what was more important still, a young girl in love.

It wasn't the wild, surging thing it had been when she met Dale Belter. It wasn't even the usual stereotype of moonlight-on-the-water generally associated with a tropical cruise.

Sam Loomis was a good ten years older than Dale Belter had been, and pretty much on the quiet side, but she loved him. It looked like the first real opportunity of all, until Sam explained a few things.

'I'm really sailing under false pretenses, you might say,' he told her. 'There's this hardware store, you see — '

Then the story had come out.

There was this hardware store, in a little town called Fairvale, up north. Sam had worked there for his father, with the understanding that he'd inherit the business. A year ago his father had died, and the accountants had told him the bad news.

Sam inherited the business, all right, plus about twenty thousand in debts. The building was mortgaged, the inventory was mortgaged, and even the insurance had been mortgaged. Sam's father had never told him about his little side investments in the market — or the race track. But there it was. There were only two choices: go into bankruptcy or try and work off the obligations.

Sam Loomis chose the latter course. 'It's a good business,' he explained. 'I'll never make a fortune, but with any kind of decent management, there's a steady eight or ten thousand a year to be made. And if I can work up a decent line of farm machinery, maybe even more. Got over four thousand paid off already. I figure another couple of years and I'll be clear.'

'But I don't understand — if you're in debt, then how can you afford to take a trip like this?'

Sam grinned at her. 'I won it in a contest. That's right — a dealer's sales contest sponsored by one of these farm-machinery outfits. I wasn't trying to win a trip at all, just hustling to pay off creditors. But they notified me I'd copped first prize in my territory.

'I tried to settle for a cash deal instead, but they wouldn't go for it. Trip or nothing. Well, this is a slack month, and I've got an honest clerk working for me. I figured I might as well take a free vacation. So here I am. And here *you* are.' He grinned, then sighed. 'I wish it was our honeymoon.'

'Sam, why *couldn't* it be? I mean — '

But he sighed again and shook his head. 'We'll have to wait. It may take two-three years before everything is paid off.'

18

'I don't want to wait! I don't care about the money. I could quit my job, work in your store — '

'And sleep in it too, the way I do?' He managed a grin again, but it was no more cheerful than the sigh. 'That's right. Rigged up a place for myself in the back room. I'm living on baked beans most of the time. Folks say I'm tighter than the town banker.'

'But what's the point?' Mary asked. 'I mean, if you lived decently it would only take a year or so longer to pay off what you owe. And meanwhile — '

'Meanwhile, I have to live in Fairvale. It's a nice town, but a small one. Everybody knows everybody else's business. As long as I'm in there pitching, I've got their respect. They go out of their way to trade with me — they all know the situation and appreciate I'm trying to do my best. Dad had a good reputation, in spite of the way things turned out. I want to keep that for myself and for the business. And for us, in the future. Now that's more important than ever. Don't you see?'

'The future.' Mary sighed. 'Two or three years, you said.'

'I'm sorry. But when we get married I want us to have a decent home, nice things. That costs money. At least you need credit. As it is, I'm stretching payments with suppliers all down the line — they'll play ball as long as they know everything I make goes toward paying off what I owe them. It isn't easy and it isn't pleasant. But I know what I want, and I can't settle for less. So you'll just have to be patient, darling.'

So she was patient. But not until she learned that no amount of further persuasion — verbal or physical — would sway him.

There the situation stood when the cruise ended. And there it had remained, for well over a year. Mary had driven up to visit him last summer; she saw the town, the store, the fresh figures in the ledger which showed that Sam had paid off an additional five thousand dollars. 'Only eleven thousand to go,' he told her proudly. 'Another two years, maybe even less.'

Two years. In two years, she'd be twenty-nine. She couldn't afford to pull a bluff, stage a scene and walk out on him like some young girl of twenty. She knew there wouldn't be many more Sam Loomises in her life. So she smiled, and nodded, and went back home to the Lowery Agency.

She went back to the Lowery Agency and watched old man Lowery take his steady five per cent on every sale he made. She watched him buy up shaky mortgages and foreclose, watched him make quick, cunning, cutthroat cash offers to desperate sellers and then turn around and take a fat profit on a fast, easy resale. People were always buying, always selling. All Lowery did was stand in the middle, extracting a percentage from both parties just for bringing buyer and seller together. He performed no other real service to justify his existence. And yet he was rich. It wouldn't take *him* two years to sweat out an eleven-thousand-dollar debt. He could sometimes make as much in two months.

Mary hated him, and she hated a lot of the buyers and sellers he did business with, because they were rich, too. This Tommy Cassidy was one of the worst — a big operator, loaded with money from oil leases. He didn't have to turn a hand, but he was always dabbling in real estate, sniffing the scent of somebody's fear or want, bidding low and selling high, alert to every possibility of squeezing out an extra dollar in rentals or income.

He thought nothing of laying down forty thousand dollars in cash to buy his daughter a home for a wedding present.

Any more than he thought anything about laying down a hundred-dollar bill on Mary Crane's desk one afternoon about six months ago, and suggesting she take a 'little trip' with him down to Dallas for the weekend.

It had all been done so quickly, and with such a bland and casual smirk, that she didn't have time to get angry. Then Mr. Lowery came in, and the matter ended. She'd never told Cassidy off, in public or in private, and he never repeated the offer. But she didn't forget. She couldn't forget the wet-lipped smile on his fat old face.

And she never forgot that this world belonged to the Tommy Cassidys. They owned the property and they set the prices. Forty thousand to a daughter for a wedding gift; a hundred dollars tossed carelessly on a desk for three days' rental privileges of the body of Mary Crane.

So I took the forty thousand dollars —

That's the way the old gag went, but this hadn't been a gag. She did take the money, and subconsciously she must have been daydreaming about just such an opportunity for a long, long time. Because now everything seemed to fall into place, as though part of a preconceived plan.

It was Friday afternoon; the banks would be closed tomorrow and that meant Lowery wouldn't get around to checking on her activities until Monday, when she didn't show up at the office.

Better still, Lila had departed, early in the morning, for Dallas — she did all the buying

22

for the record shop now. And she wouldn't be back until Monday either.

Mary drove right to the apartment and packed; not everything, just her best clothes in the suitcase and the small overnight bag. She and Lila had three hundred and sixty dollars hidden away in an empty cold-cream jar, but she didn't touch that. Lila would need it when she had to keep up the apartment alone. Mary wished that she could write her sister a note of some kind, but she didn't dare. It would be hard for Lila in the days ahead; still, there was no help for it. Maybe something could be worked out later on.

Mary left the apartment around seven; an hour later she halted on the outskirts of a suburb and ate supper, then drove in under an OK USED CARS sign and traded her sedan for a coupé. She lost money on the transaction; lost still more early the next morning when she repeated the performance in a town four hundred miles north. Around noon, when she traded again, she found herself in possession of thirty dollars in cash and a battered old heap with a crumpled left front fender, but she was not displeased. The important thing was to make a number of fast switches, cover her trail, and wind up with a junker that would take her as far as Fairvale.

Once there she could drive further north, maybe as far as Springfield, and sell the last car under her name; how would the authorities trace down the whereabouts of a Mrs. Sam Loomis, living in a town a hundred miles from there?

Because she intended to become Mrs. Sam Loomis, and quickly. She'd walk in on Sam with this story about coming into the inheritance. Not forty thousand dollars — that would be too large a sum, and might require too much explanation — but maybe she'd say it was fifteen. And she'd tell him Lila had received an equal amount, quit her job abruptly, and gone off to Europe. That would explain why there was no sense inviting her to the wedding.

Maybe Sam would balk about taking the money, and certainly there'd be a lot of awkward questions to answer, but she'd get around him. She'd have to. They'd be married at once; that was the important thing. She'd have his name, then Mrs. Sam Loomis, wife of the proprietor of a hardware store in a town eight hundred miles away from the Lowery Agency.

The Lowery Agency didn't even know of Sam's existence. Of course they'd come to Lila, and she'd probably guess right away. But Lila wouldn't say anything — not until she contacted Mary first.

When that time came, Mary would have to be prepared to handle her sister, keep her quiet in front of Sam and the authorities. It shouldn't be too difficult — Lila owed her that much, for all the years Mary had worked to send her through school. Perhaps she could even give her part of the remaining twenty-five thousand dollars. Maybe she wouldn't take it. But there would be some solution; Mary hadn't planned that far ahead, but when the time came, the answer would be ready.

Right now she had to do one thing at a time, and the first step was to reach Fairvale. On the scale map it was a distance of a mere four inches. Four insignificant inches of red lines from one dot to another. But it had taken her eighteen hours to get this far; eighteen hours of endless vibration, eighteen hours of peering and squinting in headlight glare and sunlight reflection; eighteen hours of cramped contortion, of fighting the road and the wheel and the dulling, deadly onslaught of her own fatigue.

Now she had missed her turn and it was raining; the night had come down and she was lost, on a strange road.

Mary glanced into the rear-view mirror and caught a dim reflection of her face. The dark hair and the regular features were still familiar, but the smile had gone and her full lips were compressed to a taut line. Where had she seen that drawn, contorted countenance before?

In the mirror after Mom died, when you went to pieces —

And here, all along, she'd thought of herself as being so calm, so cool, so composed. There had been no consciousness of fear, of regret, of guilt. But the mirror didn't lie. It told her the truth now.

It told her, wordlessly, to *stop. You can't stumble into Sam's arms looking like this, coming out of the night with your face and clothing giving away the story of hasty flight. Sure, your story is that you wanted to surprise him with the good news, but you'll have to look as though you're so happy you couldn't wait.*

The thing to do was to stay over somewhere tonight, get a decent rest, and arrive in Fairvale tomorrow morning, alert and refreshed.

If she turned around and drove back to the place where she made the wrong turnoff, she'd hit the main highway again. Then she could find a motel.

Mary nodded to herself, resisting the impulse to close her eyes, and then jerked

26

erect, scanning the side of the road through the blur of rainswept darkness.

That's when she saw the sign, set beside the driveway which led to the small building off on the side.

MOTEL — VACANCY. The sign was unlit, but maybe they'd forgotten to switch it on, just as she'd forgotten to put on her head-lights when the night suddenly descended.

Mary drove in, noting that the entire motel was dark, including the glass-front cubicle on the end which undoubtedly served as an office. Maybe the place was closed. She slowed down and peered in, then felt her tires roll over one of those electric signal cables. Now she could see the house on the hillside behind the motel; its front windows were lighted, and probably the proprietor was up there. He'd come down in a moment.

She switched off the ignition and waited. All at once she could hear the sullen patter of the rain and sense the sigh of the wind behind it. She remembered the sound, because it had rained like that the day Mom was buried, the day they lowered her into that little rectangle of darkness. And now the darkness was here, rising all around Mary. She was alone in the dark. The money wouldn't help her and Sam wouldn't help her, because she'd taken the wrong turn back there and she was on a strange road. But no help for it — she'd made her grave and now she must lie in it.

Why did she think that? It wasn't *grave*, it was *bed*.

She was still trying to puzzle it out when the big dark shadow emerged out of the other shadows and opened her car door.

3

'Looking for a room?'

Mary made up her mind very quickly, once she saw the fat, bespectacled face and heard the soft, hesitant voice. There wouldn't be any trouble.

She nodded and climbed out of the car, feeling the ache in her calves as she followed him to the door of the office. He unlocked it, stepped inside the cubicle and switched on the light.

'Sorry I didn't get down sooner. I've been up at the house — Mother isn't very well.'

There was nothing distinctive about the office, but it was warm and dry and bright. Mary shivered gratefully and smiled up at the fat man. He bent over the ledger on the counter.

'Our rooms are seven dollars, single. Would you like to take a look, first?'

'That won't be necessary.' She opened her purse quickly, extracting a five-dollar bill and two singles and placing them on the counter as he pushed the register forward and held out a pen.

For a moment she hesitated, then wrote a

29

name — *Jane Wilson* — and an address — *San Antonio, Texas*. She couldn't very well do anything about the Texas plates on the car.

'I'll get your bags,' he said, and came around the counter. She followed him outside again. The money was in the glove compartment, still in the same big envelope secured by the heavy rubber band. Maybe the best thing to do was to leave it there; she'd lock the car, and nobody would disturb it.

He carried the bags over to the door of the room next to the office. It was the closest, and she didn't mind — the main thing was to get out of the rain.

'Nasty weather,' he said, standing aside as she entered. 'Have you been driving long?'

'All day.'

He pressed a switch and the bedside lamp blossomed and sent forth yellow petals of light. The room was plainly but adequately furnished; she noted the shower stall in the bathroom beyond. Actually, she would have preferred a tub, but this would do.

'Everything all right?'

She nodded quickly, then remembered something. 'Is there anywhere around here where I can get a bite to eat?'

'Well, let's see, now. There used to be a root beer and hamburger stand up the road here about three miles, but I guess it's closed down now since the new highway came in. No, your best bet would be Fairvale.'

'How far away is that?'

'About seventeen-eighteen miles. You keep going up the road until you come to a county trunk, turn right, and hit the main highway again. It's ten miles straight ahead, then. I'm surprised you didn't go through that way if you're heading north.'

'I got lost.'

The fat man nodded and sighed. 'I thought as much. We don't get much regular traffic along here any more since that new road opened.'

She smiled absently. He stood in the doorway, pursing his lips. When she looked up to meet his stare, he dropped his eyes and cleared his throat apologetically.

'Uh — Miss — I was just thinking. Maybe you don't feel like driving all the way up to Fairvale and back in this rain. I mean, I was just going to fix a little snack for myself up at the house. You'd be perfectly welcome to join me.'

'Oh, I couldn't do that.'

'Why not? No trouble at all. Mother's gone back to bed, and she won't be doing any cooking — I was only going to set out some cold cuts and make some coffee. If that's all right with you.'

'Well — '

'Look, I'll just run along and get things ready.'

'Thank you very much, Mr. — '

'Bates. Norman Bates.' He backed against the door, bumping his shoulder. 'Look, I'll leave you this flashlight for when you come up. You probably want to get out of those wet things first.'

He turned away, but not before she caught a glimpse of his reddened face. Why, he was actually *embarrassed!*

For the first time in almost twenty hours a smile came to Mary Crane's face. She waited until the door closed behind him and then slipped out of her jacket. She opened her overnight bag on the bed and took out a print dress. She let it hang, hoping some of the wrinkles would disappear, while she used the bathroom facilities. Just time to freshen up a bit now, but when she came back she promised herself a good hot shower. That's what she needed; that, and sleep. But first a little food. Let's see, now — her make-up was in her purse, and she could wear the blue coat from the big suitcase —

Fifteen minutes later she was knocking on the door of the big frame house on the hillside.

A single lamp shone from the unshaded

parlor window, but a brighter reflection blazed from upstairs. If his mother was ill, that's where she'd be.

Mary stood there, waiting for a response, but nothing happened. Maybe he was upstairs, too. She rapped again.

Meanwhile, she peered through the parlor window. At first glance she couldn't quite believe what she saw; she hadn't dreamed that such places still existed in this day and age.

Usually, even when a house is old, there are some signs of alteration and improvement in the interior. But the parlor she peered at had never been 'modernized'; the floral wallpaper, the dark, heavy, ornately scrolled mahogany woodwork, the turkey-red carpet, the highbacked, overstuffed furniture and the paneled fireplace were straight out of the Gay Nineties. There wasn't even a television set to intrude its incongruity in the scene, but she did notice an old wind-up gramophone on an end table. Now she could detect a low murmur of voices, and at first she thought it might be coming from the gramophone's bell-shaped horn; then she identified the source of the sound. It was coming from upstairs, from the lighted room.

Mary knocked again, using the end of the

flashlight. This time she must have made her presence known, for the sound ceased abruptly, and she heard the faint thud of footsteps. A moment later she saw Mr. Bates descending the stairs. He came to the door and opened it, gesturing her forward.

'Sorry,' he said. 'I was just tucking Mother in for the night. Sometimes she's apt to be a bit difficult.'

'You said she was ill. I wouldn't want to disturb her.'

'Oh, you won't make any bother. She'll probably sleep like a baby.' Mr. Bates glanced over his shoulder at the stairway, then lowered his voice. 'Actually, she's not sick, not *physically*, that is. But sometimes she gets these spells — '

He nodded abruptly, then smiled. 'Here, let me just take your coat and hang it up. There. Now, if you'll come this way — '

She followed him down a hallway which extended from under the stairs. 'I hope you don't mind eating in the kitchen,' he murmured. 'Everything's all ready for us. Sit right down and I'll pour the coffee.'

The kitchen was a complement of the parlor — lined with ceiling-high glassed-in cupboards grouped about an old-fashioned sink with a hand-pump attachment. The big wood stove squatted in one corner. But it gave off a grateful warmth, and the long wooden table bore a welcome display of sausage, cheese and homemade pickles in glass dishes scattered about on the red-and-white checkered cloth. Mary was not inclined to smile at the quaintness of it all, and even the inevitable hand-crocheted motto on the wall seemed appropriate enough.

God Bless Our Home.

So be it. This was a lot better than sitting alone in some dingy small-town cafeteria.

Mr. Bates helped her fill her plate. 'Go right ahead, don't wait for me! You must be hungry.'

She *was* hungry, and she ate heartily, with such absorption that she scarcely noticed how little he was eating. When she became aware of it, she was faintly embarrassed.

'But you haven't touched a thing! I'll bet you really had your own supper earlier.'

'No, I didn't. It's just that I'm not very hungry.' He refilled her coffee cup. 'I'm afraid Mother gets me a little upset sometimes.' His voice lowered again, and the apologetic note returned. 'I guess it's my fault. I'm not too good at taking care of her.'

'You live here all alone, the two of you?'

'Yes. There's never been anybody else. Never.'

'It must be pretty hard on you.'

'I'm not complaining. Don't misunder-stand.' He adjusted the rimless spectacles. 'My father went away when I was still a baby. Mother took care of me all alone. There was enough money on her side of the family to keep us going, I guess, until I grew up. Then she mortgaged the house, sold the farm land, and built this motel. We ran it together, and it was a good thing — until the new highway cut us off.

'Actually, of course, she started failing long before then. And it was my turn to take care of her. But sometimes it isn't so easy.'

'There are no other relatives?'

'None.'

'And you've never married?'

His face reddened and he glanced down at the checkered tablecloth.

Mary bit her lip. 'I'm sorry. I didn't mean to ask personal questions.'

'That's all right.' His voice was faint. 'I've never married. Mother was — funny — about those things. I — I've never even sat at a table with a girl like this before.'

'But — '

'Sounds odd, doesn't it, in this day and age? I know that. But it has to be. I tell myself that she'd be lost without me, now — but maybe the real truth is that *I'd* be even more lost without *her*.'

Mary finished her coffee, fished in her purse for cigarettes, and offered the package to Mr. Bates.

'No, thank you. I don't smoke.'

'Mind if I do?'

'Not at all. Go right ahead.' He hesitated. 'I'd like to offer you a drink but — you see — Mother doesn't approve of liquor in the house.'

Mary leaned back, inhaling. Suddenly she felt expansive. Funny what a little warmth, a little rest, a little food could do. An hour ago she'd been lonely, wretched, and fearfully unsure of herself. Now everything had changed. Perhaps it was listening to Mr. Bates which had altered her mood this way. *He* was the lonely, wretched, and fearful one, really. In contrast, she felt seven feet tall. It was this realization which prompted her to speak.

'You aren't allowed to smoke. You aren't allowed to drink. You aren't allowed to see any girls. Just what *do* you do, besides run the motel and attend to your mother?'

Apparently he was unconscious of her tone of voice. 'Oh, I've got lots of things to do, really. I read quite a bit. And there are other hobbies.' He glanced up at a wall shelf and she followed his gaze. A stuffed squirrel peered down at them.

37

'Hunting?'

'Well, no. Just taxidermy. George Blount gave me that squirrel to stuff. He shot it. Mother doesn't want me to handle firearms.'

'Mr. Bates, you'll pardon me for saying this, but how long do you intend to go on this way? You're a grown man. You certainly must realize that you can't be expected to act like a little boy all the rest of your life. I don't mean to be rude, but — '

'I understand. I'm well aware of the situation. As I told you, I've done a bit of reading. I know what the psychologists say about such things. But I have a duty toward my mother.'

'Wouldn't you perhaps be fulfilling that duty to her, and to yourself as well, if you arranged to put her in an — institution?'

'*She's not crazy!*'

The voice wasn't soft and apologetic any longer; it was high and shrill. And the pudgy man was on his feet, his hands sweeping a cup from the table. It shattered on the floor, but Mary didn't look at it; she could only stare into the shattered face.

'She's not crazy,' he repeated. 'No matter what you think, or anybody thinks. No matter what the books say, or what those doctors would say out at the asylum. I know all about that. They'd certify her in a hurry and lock

38

her away if they could — all I'd have to do is give them the word. But I wouldn't, because I *know*. Don't you understand that? I *know*, and they don't know. They don't know how she took care of me all those years, when there was nobody else who cared, how she worked for me and suffered because of me, the sacrifices she made. If she's a little odd now, it's my fault, I'm responsible. When she came to me that time, told me she wanted to get married again, I'm the one who stopped her. Yes, I stopped her, I was to blame for that! You don't have to tell me about jealousy, possessiveness — I was worse than she could ever be. Ten times crazier, if that's the word you want to use. They'd have locked *me* up in a minute if they knew the things I said and did, the way I carried on. Well, I got over it, finally. And she didn't. But who are you to say a person should be put away? I think perhaps all of us go a little crazy at times.'

He stopped, not because he was out of words but because he was out of breath. His face was very red, and the puckered lips were beginning to tremble.

Mary stood up. 'I'm — I'm sorry,' she said softly. 'Really, I am. I want to apologize. I had no right to say what I did.'

'Yes. I know. But it doesn't matter. It's just that I'm not used to talking about these

39

things. You live alone like this and everything gets bottled up. Bottled up, or stuffed, like that squirrel up there.'

His color lightened, and he attempted a smile. 'Cute little fellow, isn't he? I've often wished I had a live one around that I could tame for a pet.'

Mary picked up her purse. 'I'll be running along now. It's getting late.'

'Please don't go. I'm sorry I made such a fuss.'

'It isn't that. I'm really very tired.'

'But I thought perhaps we could talk awhile. I was going to tell you about my hobbies. I've got a sort of a workshop down in the basement — '

'No, I'd like to, but I simply must get some rest.'

'All right, then. I'll walk down with you. I've got to close up the office. It doesn't look as if there'll be any more business tonight.'

They went through the hall, and he helped her on with her coat. He was clumsy about it, and for a moment she felt rising irritation, then checked it as she realized the cause. He was afraid to touch her. That was it. The poor guy was actually afraid to get near a woman!

He held the flashlight and she followed him out of the house and down the pathway to the gravel drive curving around the motel. The rain had stopped but the night was still dark and starless. As she turned the corner of the building she glanced back over her shoulder at the house. The upstairs light still burned, and Mary wondered if the old woman was awake, if she had listened to their conversation, heard the final outburst.

Mr. Bates halted before her door, waited until she inserted the key in the lock and opened it.

'Good night,' he said. 'Sleep well.'

'Thank you. And thanks for the hospitality.'

He opened his mouth, then turned away. For the third time that evening she saw him redden.

Then she closed her door and locked it. She could hear his retreating footsteps, then the telltale click as he entered the office next door.

She didn't hear him when he left; her attention had been immediately occupied by the duty of unpacking. She got out her pajamas, her slippers, a jar of cold cream, a toothbrush and toothpaste. Then she rummaged through the big suitcase looking for the dress she planned to wear tomorrow, when she saw Sam. That would have to be put up now, to hang out the wrinkles. Nothing must be out of place tomorrow.

Nothing must be out of place —

All at once she didn't feel seven feet tall any more. Or was the change really so sudden? Hadn't it started when Mr. Bates got so hysterical, back there at the house? What was it he had said which really deflated her?

I think perhaps all of us go a little crazy at times.

Mary Crane cleared a place for herself on the bed and sat down.

Yes. It was true. All of us go a little crazy at times. Just as she'd gone crazy, yesterday afternoon, when she saw that money on the desk.

And she'd been crazy ever since, she *must* have been crazy, to think she could get away with what she planned. It had all seemed like a dream come true, and that's what it was. A dream. A *crazy* dream. She knew it, now.

Maybe she could manage to throw off the police. But Sam would ask questions. *Who* was this relative she'd inherited the money from? *Where* had he lived? Why hadn't she ever mentioned him before? How was it that she brought the money along in cash? Didn't Mr. Lowery object to her quitting her job so suddenly?

And then there was Lila. Suppose she reacted as Mary had anticipated — came to her without going to the police, even consented to remain silent in the future because of a sense of obligation. The fact remained that she'd *know*. And there'd be complications.

Sooner or later Sam would want to visit her down there, or invite her up. And that would never work. She could never keep up a future relationship with her sister; never explain to Sam why it was impossible to do so, why she wouldn't go back to Texas even for a visit.

No, the whole thing was crazy.

And it was too late to do anything about it now.

Or — *was it?*

Suppose she got herself some sleep, a good long ten hours of sleep. Tomorrow was Sunday; if she left here about nine and drove straight through she could be back in town Monday morning, early. Before Lila arrived from Dallas, before the bank opened. She could deposit the money and go on to work from there.

Sure, she'd be dead tired. But it wouldn't kill her, and nobody would ever know.

There was the matter of the car, of course. That would take some explaining, for Lila's benefit. Maybe she could tell her that she'd started out for Fairvale, intending to surprise Sam over the weekend. The car broke down and she had to have it towed away — the dealer said it would need a new engine, so she decided to junk it, take this old heap instead, and come back home.

Yes, that would sound reasonable.

Of course, when she figured everything up, this trip would actually cost her about seven hundred dollars. That's what the car had been worth.

But the price was worth paying. Seven hundred dollars isn't too much to pay for one's sanity. For one's safety, one's future security.

Mary stood up.

She'd do it.

And all at once she was seven feet tall again. It was *that* simple.

If she'd been a religious girl, she would have prayed. As it was, she felt a curious sense of — what was that word? — predestination. As if everything that had happened was somehow *fated* to be. Her turning off on the wrong road, coming here, meeting that pathetic man, listening to his outburst, hearing that final sentence which brought her to her senses.

For a moment, she could have gone to him and kissed him — until she realized, with a giggle, what his response would be to such a gesture. The poor old geezer would probably faint!

She giggled again. It was nice to be seven

feet tall, but the question was — would she be able to fit inside the shower stall? And that's what she was going to do right now, take a nice, long hot shower. Get the dirt off her hide, just as she was going to get the dirt cleaned out of her insides. *Come clean, Mary. Come clean as snow.*

She stepped into the bathroom, kicking off her shoes, stooping to slip her stockings off. Then she raised her arms, pulled the dress over her head, tossed it into the next room. It missed the bed, but she didn't care. She unhooked her bra, swung it in an arc, and let it sail. Now, the panties —

For a moment she stood before the mirror set in the door and took stock of herself. Maybe the face was twenty-seven, but the body was free, white, and twenty-one. She had a good figure. A *damned* good figure. Sam would like it. She wished he was here to admire it now. It was going to be hell to wait another two years. But then she'd make up for lost time. They say a woman isn't fully mature, sexually, until she's thirty. That was something to find out about.

Mary giggled again, then executed an amateurish bump and grind, tossed her image a kiss and received one in return. After that she stepped into the shower stall. The water was hot, and she had to add a mixture from the COLD faucet. Finally she turned both faucets on full force and let the warmth gush over her.

The roar was deafening, and the room was beginning to steam up.

That's why she didn't hear the door open, or note the sound of footsteps. And at first, when the shower curtains parted, the steam obscured the face.

Then she *did* see it there — just a face, peering through the curtains, hanging in midair like a mask. A head-scarf concealed the hair and the glassy eyes stared inhumanly, but it wasn't a mask, it couldn't be. The skin had been powdered dead-white and two hectic spots of rouge centered on the cheekbones. It wasn't a mask. It was the face of a crazy old woman.

Mary started to scream, and then the curtains parted further and a hand appeared, holding a butcher knife. It was the knife that, a moment later, cut off her scream.

And her head.

4

The minute Norman got inside the office he started to tremble. It was the reaction, of course. Too much had happened, and too quickly. He couldn't bottle it up any longer.

Bottle. That's what he needed — a drink. He'd lied to the girl, of course. It was true Mother wouldn't allow liquor in the house, but he *did* drink. He kept a bottle down here, at the office. There were times when you had to drink, even if you knew you had no stomach for liquor, even if a few ounces were enough to make you dizzy, make you pass out. There were times when you *wanted* to pass out.

Norman remembered to pull down the venetian blinds and switch off the sign outside. There, that did it. Closed for the night. Nobody would notice the dim light of the desk lamp now that the blinds were down. Nobody could look in and see him opening the desk drawer and pulling out the bottle, his hands trembling like a baby's. *Baby needs his bottle.*

He tilted the pint back and drank, closing his eyes as he did so. The whisky burned, and that was good. Let it burn away the bitterness. The warmth crept down his throat, exploded in his stomach. Maybe another drink would burn away the taste of fear.

It had been a mistake to invite the girl up to the house. Norman knew that the moment he opened his mouth, but she was so pretty, and she had looked so tired and forlorn. He knew what it was to be tired and forlorn, with nobody to turn to, nobody, who'd understand. All he meant to do, all he did do, was talk to her. Besides, it was *his* house, wasn't it? Just as much as it was Mother's. She had no right to lay down the law that way.

Still, it had been a mistake. Actually, he never would have dared, except that he'd been so angry with Mother. He'd wanted to defy her. That was bad.

But he had done something far worse after he extended the invitation. He'd gone back to the house and told Mother he was having company. He'd marched right up to the bedroom and announced it, just as much as to say, 'I dare you to do something about it!'

It was the wrong thing to do. She was worked up enough already, and when he told her about the girl coming for supper she practically had hysterics. She *was* hysterical, the way she carried on, the things she said. 'If you bring her here, I'll kill her! I'll kill the bitch!'

Bitch. Mother didn't talk that way. But that's what she had said. She was sick, very sick. Maybe the girl had been right. Maybe Mother should be put away. It was getting so he couldn't handle her alone any more. Getting so he couldn't handle himself, either. What had Mother used to say about handling himself? It was a sin. You could burn in hell.

The whisky burned. His third drink, but he needed it. He needed a lot of things. The girl was right about that, too. This was no way to live. He couldn't go on much longer.

Just getting through the meal had been an ordeal. He'd been afraid Mother would make a scene. After he locked the door to her room and left her up there he kept wondering if she'd start screaming and pounding. But she had kept very quiet, almost too quiet, as though she was listening. Probably that's just what she had been doing. You could lock Mother up, but you couldn't keep her from listening.

Norman hoped she'd gone to sleep by now. Tomorrow she might forget the whole episode. That often happened. And then again, sometimes when he thought she had completely forgotten an incident, she'd bring

49

it up out of a clear blue sky, months afterward.

Clear blue sky. He chuckled at the phrase. There weren't any clear blue skies any more. Just clouds and darkness, like tonight.

Then he heard a sound, and he shifted quickly in his chair. Was Mother coming? No, it couldn't be, he'd locked her up, remember? It must be that girl, in the next room. Yes, he could hear her now — she'd opened her suitcase, apparently, and she was taking things out, getting ready for bed.

Norman took another drink. Just to steady his nerves. And this time it worked. His hand wasn't trembling any more. He wasn't afraid. Not if he thought about the girl.

Funny, when he actually saw her, he had this terrible feeling of — what was the word? *Im*-something. *Importance.* No, that wasn't it. He didn't feel important when he was with a woman. He felt — *impossible?* That wasn't right, either. He knew the word he was looking for, he'd read it a hundred times in books, the kind of books Mother didn't even know he owned.

Well, it didn't matter. When he was with the girl he felt that way, but not now. Now he could do anything

And there were so many things he wanted to do with a girl like that. Young, pretty;

intelligent, too. He'd made a fool of himself answering her back when she talked about Mother; now he admitted she had told the truth. She knew, she could understand. He wished she would have stayed and talked more.

As it was, maybe he'd never see her again. Tomorrow she'd be gone. Gone forever. Jane Wilson, of San Antonio, Texas. He wondered who she was, where she was going, what kind of a *person* she really was, inside. He could fall in love with a girl like that. Yes, he could, after just seeing her a single time. It was nothing to laugh at. But she'd laugh, probably. That's the way girls were — they always laughed. Because they were bitches.

Mother was right. They were bitches. But you couldn't help yourself, not when a bitch was as lovely as this one was, and you knew you would never see her again. You *had* to see her again. If you were any kind of a man, you'd have told her so, when you were in her room. You'd have brought in the bottle and offered her a drink, drunk with her, and then you'd carry her over to the bed and — No, you wouldn't. Not *you*. Because you're impotent.

That's the word you couldn't remember, isn't it? *Impotent*. The word the books used, the word Mother used, the word that meant you were never going to see her again because it wouldn't do any good. The word the bitches knew; they must know it, and that's why they always laughed.

Norman took another drink, just a sip. He could feel the wetness trickle down the side of his chin. He must be drunk. All right, he was drunk, what did it matter? As long as Mother didn't know. As long as the girl didn't know. It would all be a big secret. Impotent, was he? Well, that didn't mean he couldn't see her again.

He was going to see her, right now.

Norman bent forward across the desk, his head inclined and almost touching the wall. He'd heard more sounds. And from long experience he knew how to interpret them. The girl had kicked off her shoes. Now she was coming into the bathroom.

He reached out his hand. It was trembling again, but not with fear. This was anticipation; he knew what he was going to do. He was going to tilt the framed license on the wall to one side and peek through the little hole he'd drilled so long ago. Nobody else knew about the little hole, not even Mother. Most certainly not Mother. It was his secret.

The little hole was just a crack in the plaster on the other side, but he could see through it. See through it into the lighted bathroom. Sometimes he'd catch a person standing right in front of it. Sometimes he'd catch their reflection on the door mirror beyond. But he could see. He could see plenty. Let the bitches laugh at him. He knew more about them than they ever dreamed.

It was hard for Norman to focus his eyes. He felt hot and dizzy, hot and dizzy. Part of it was due to the drinks, part to the excitement. But most of it was due to her.

She *was* in the bathroom now, standing there facing the wall. But she wouldn't notice the crack. They never did. She was smiling, fluffing out her hair. Now she stooped, sliding down her stockings. And as she straightened up, yes, she was going to do it, the dress was coming off over her head, he could see the bra and panties, she mustn't stop now, she mustn't turn away —

But she did turn away, and Norman almost called out to her, 'Come back here, you bitch!' but he remembered just in time, and then he saw that she was unhooking her bra in front of the door mirror and he could see. Except that the mirror was all wavy lines and lights that made him dizzy, and it was hard to make out anything until she stepped a little to one side. Then he could see her . . .

Now she was going to take them off, she *was* taking them off, and he could see, she

53

was standing before the mirror and actually *gesturing!*

Did she know? Had she known all along, known about the hole in the wall, known that he was watching? Did she want him to watch, was she doing this to him on purpose, the bitch? She was swaying back and forth, back and forth, and now the mirror was wavy again and she was wavy, and he couldn't stand it, he wanted to pound on the wall, he wanted to scream at her to stop because this was an evil, perverted thing she was doing and she must stop before he became evil and perverted too. That's what the bitches did to you, they perverted you, and she was a bitch, they were all bitches, Mother was a —

Suddenly she was gone, and there was only the roaring. It welled up, shaking the wall, drowning out the words and the thoughts. It was coming from inside his head, and he fell back in the chair. *I'm drunk,* he told himself. *I'm passing out.*

But that was not entirely so. The roaring continued, and somewhere inside it he heard another sound. The office door was opening. How could that be? He'd locked it, hadn't he? And he still had the key. If only he'd open his eyes, he could find it. But he couldn't open his eyes. He didn't dare. Because now he knew.

Mother had a key too.

She had a key to her room. She had a key to the house. She had a key to the office.

And she was standing there now, looking down at him. He hoped she would think he had just fallen asleep. What was she doing here, anyway? Had she heard him leave with the girl, come down to spy on him?

Norman slumped back, not daring to move, not wanting to move. Every instant it was getting harder and harder to move even if he *had* wanted to. The roaring was steady now, and the vibration was rocking him to sleep. That was nice. To be rocked to sleep, with Mother standing over you —

Then she was gone. She'd turned around without saying anything and gone out. There was nothing to be afraid of. She'd come to protect him from the bitches. Yes, that was it. She'd come to protect him. Whenever he needed her, Mother was there. And now he could sleep. There was no trick to it at all. You merely went into the roaring, and then *past* the roaring. Then everything was silent. *Sleep, silent sleep.*

Norman came to with a start, jerking his head back. God, it ached! He'd passed out there in the chair, actually passed out. No wonder everything was pounding, roaring. *Roaring.* He'd heard the same sound before.

55

How long ago — an hour, two hours?

Now he recognized it. The shower was going next door. That was it. The girl had gone into the shower. But that had been so long ago. She couldn't *still* be in there, could she?

He reached forward, tilting the framed license on the wall. His eyes squinted and then focused on the brightly lit bathroom beyond. It was empty. He couldn't see into the shower stall on the side. The curtains were closed and he couldn't see.

Maybe she'd forgotten about the shower and gone to bed leaving it turned on. It seemed odd that she'd be able to sleep with the water running full force that way, but then he'd done it himself just now. Maybe fatigue was as intoxicating as alcohol.

Anyway, there didn't seem to be anything wrong. The bathroom was in order. Norman scanned it once again, then noticed the floor.

Water from the shower was trickling across the tiles. Not much, just a little, just enough for him to see it. A tiny rivulet of water, trailing across the white tiled floor.

Or was it water? Water isn't *pink*. Water doesn't have tiny threads of red in it, tiny threads of red like veins.

She must have slipped, she must have fallen and hurt herself, Norman decided. The panic was rising in him, but he knew what he must do. He grabbed up his keys from the desk and hurried out of the office. Quickly he found the right one for the adjoining unit and opened the door. The bedroom was empty, but the open suitcase still rested on the bed itself. She hadn't gone away. So he'd guessed correctly; there'd been an accident in the shower. He'd have to go in there.

It wasn't until he actually entered the bathroom that he remembered something else, and then it was too late. The panic burst loose, but that didn't help him now. He still remembered.

Mother had keys to the motel too.

And then, as he ripped back the shower curtains and stared down at the hacked and twisted thing sprawled on the floor of the stall, he realized that Mother had used her keys.

5

Norman locked the door behind him and went up to the house. His clothes were a mess. Blood on them, of course, and water, and then he'd been sick all over the bathroom floor.

But that wasn't important now. There were other things which must be cleaned up first.

This time he was going to do something about it, once and for all. He was going to put Mother where she belonged. He had to.

All the panic, all the fear, all the horror and nausea and revulsion, gave way to this overriding resolve. What had happened was tragic, dreadful beyond words, but it would never happen again. He felt like a new man — his own man.

Norman hurried up the steps and tried the front door. It was unlocked. The light in the parlor was still burning, but it was empty. He gave a quick glance around, then mounted the stairs.

The door to Mother's room stood open, and lamplight fanned forth into the hall. He stepped in, not bothering to knock. No need to pretend any more. She couldn't get away with this.

She couldn't get away — But she had.

The bedroom was empty.

He could see the rumpled indentation where she had lain, see the covers flung back on the big fourposter; smell the faint, musty scent still in the room. The rocker rested in the corner, the ornaments stood on the dresser just as they were always arranged. Nothing had changed in Mother's room; nothing ever changed. But Mother was gone.

He stepped over to the closet, ruffling the clothing on the hangers lining the long center pole. Here the acrid scent was very strong, so strong he almost choked, but there was another odor, too. It wasn't until his foot slipped that he looked down and realized where it was coming from. One of her dresses and a head-scarf were balled up on the floor. He stooped to retrieve them, then shivered in revulsion as he noted the dark, reddish stains of clotted blood.

She'd come back here, then; come back, changed her clothes, and gone off once more.

He couldn't call the police.

That was the thing he had to remember. He mustn't call the police. Not even now, knowing what she had done. Because she wasn't really responsible. She was sick.

Cold-blooded murder is one thing, but sickness is another. You aren't really a murderer when you're sick in the head. Anybody knows that. Only sometimes the courts didn't agree. He'd read of cases. Even if they did recognize what was wrong with her, they'd still put her away. Not in a rest home, but in one of those awful holes. A state hospital.

Norman stared at the neat, old-fashioned room with its wallpaper pattern of rambler roses. He couldn't take Mother away from this and see her locked up in a bare cell. Right now he was safe — the police didn't even know about Mother. She stayed here, in the house, and *nobody* knew. It had been all right to tell the girl, because she'd never see him again. But the police couldn't find out about Mother and what she was like. They'd put her away to rot. No matter what she'd done, she didn't deserve *that*.

And she wouldn't have to get it, because nobody knew what she'd done.

He was pretty certain, now, that he could keep anyone from knowing. All he had to do was think it over, think back to the events of the evening, think carefully.

The girl had driven in alone, said she'd been on the road all day. That meant she wasn't visiting *en route*. And she didn't seem to know where Fairvale was, didn't mention any other towns nearby, so the chances were she had no intention of seeing anyone around here. Whoever expected her — if anyone *was* expecting her — must live some distance further north.

Of course this was all supposition, but it seemed logical enough. And he'd have to take a chance on being right.

She had signed the register, of course, but that meant nothing. If anybody ever asked, he'd say that she had spent the night and driven on.

All he had to do was get rid of the body and the car and make sure that everything was cleaned up afterward.

That part would be easy. He knew just how to do it. It wouldn't be pleasant, but it wouldn't be difficult, either.

And it would save him from going to the police. It would save Mother.

Oh, he still intended to have things out with her — he wasn't backing down on that part of it, not this time — but this could wait until afterward.

The big thing now was to dispose of the evidence. The *corpus delicti*.

Mother's dress and scarf would have to be burned, and so would the clothing he was wearing. No, on second thought, he might as well get rid of it all when he got rid of the body.

Norman wadded the garments into a ball and carried them downstairs. He grabbed an old shirt and a pair of coveralls from the hook in the back hallway, then shed his clothing in the kitchen and donned the others. No sense stopping to wash up now — that could wait until the rest of the messy business was completed.

But Mother had remembered to wash when she came back. He could see more of the pink stains here at the kitchen sink; a few telltale traces of rouge and powder, too.

He made a mental note to clean everything thoroughly when he got back, then sat down and transferred everything from the pockets of his discarded clothing to those in his coveralls. It was a pity to throw away good clothes like this, but that couldn't be helped. Not if Mother was to be helped.

Norman went down into the basement and opened the door of the old fruit cellar. He found what he was looking for — a discarded clothes hamper with a sprung cover. It was large enough and it would do nicely.

Nicely — God, how can you think like that about what you're proposing to do?

He winced at the realization, then took a deep breath. This was no time to be self-conscious or self-critical. One had to be practical. Very practical, very careful, very calm.

Calmly, he tossed his clothes into the hamper. Calmly, he took an old oilcloth from the table near the cellar stairs. Calmly, he went back upstairs, snapped off the kitchen light, snapped off the hall light, and let himself out of the house in darkness, carrying the hamper with the oilcloth on top.

It was harder to be calm here in the dark. Harder not to think about a hundred and one things that might go wrong.

Mother had wandered off — where? Was she out on the highway, ready to be picked up by anyone who might come driving by? Was she still suffering a hysterical reaction, would the shock of what she had done cause her to blurt out the truth to whoever came along and found her? Had she actually run away, or was she merely in a daze? Maybe she'd gone down past the woods back of the house, along the narrow ten-acre strip of their land which stretched off into the swamp. Wouldn't it be better to search for her first?

Norman sighed and shook his head. He couldn't afford the risk. Not while that thing still sprawled in the shower stall back at the motel. Leaving it there was even more risky.

He'd had the presence of mind to turn off

all the lights, both in the office and in her room, before leaving. But even so, one never knew when some night owl might show up and nose around looking for accommodations. It didn't happen very often, but every once in a while the signal would buzz; sometimes at one or two o'clock in the morning. And at least once in the course of a night the State Highway Patrol car cruised past here. It almost never stopped, but there was the chance.

He stumbled along in the pitch blackness of moonless midnight. The path was graveled and not muddy, but the rain would have softened the ground behind the house. There'd be tracks. That was something else to think about. He'd leave tracks he couldn't even see. If only it wasn't so dark! All at once that was the most important thing — to get out of the dark.

Norman was very grateful when he finally opened the door of the girl's room and eased the hamper inside, then set it down and switched on the light. The soft glow reassured him for a moment, until he remembered what the light would reveal when he went into the bathroom.

He stood in the center of the bedroom now, and he began to tremble.

No, I can't do it. I can't look at her. I

won't go in there. I won't!

But you have to. There's no other way. And stop talking to yourself!

That was the most important thing. He had to stop talking to himself. He had to get back that calm feeling again. He had to face reality.

And what was reality?

A dead girl. The girl his mother had killed. Not a pretty sight nor a pretty notion, but there it was.

Walking away wouldn't bring the girl back to life again. Turning Mother in to the police wouldn't help alter the situation either. The best thing to do under the circumstances, the *only* thing to do, was to get rid of her. He needn't feel guilty about it.

But he couldn't hold back his nausea, his dizziness, and his dry, convulsive retching when it came to actually going into the shower stall and doing what must be done there. He found the butcher knife almost at once; it was under the torso. He dropped *that* into the hamper immediately. There was an old pair of gloves in his coverall pockets; he had to put them on before he could bring himself to touch the rest. The head was the worst. Nothing else was severed, only slashed, and he had to fold the limbs before he could wrap the body in the oilcloth and crowd it down into the hamper on top of the clothing.

Then it was done, and he slammed the lid shut.

That still left the bathroom and the shower stall itself to be cleaned up, but he'd deal with that part of the job when he came back.

Now he had to lug the hamper out into the bedroom, then put it down while he found the girl's purse and ransacked it for her car keys. He opened the door slowly, scanning the road for passing headlights. Nothing was coming — nothing had come this way for hours. He could only hope and pray that nothing *would* come, now.

He was sweating long before he managed to open the trunk of the car and place the hamper inside; sweating, not with exertion, but with fear. But he made it, and then he was back in the room again, picking up the clothing and shoving it into the overnight bag and the big suitcase on the bed. He found the shoes, the stockings, the bra, the panties. Touching the bra and panties was the worst. If there'd been anything left in his stomach it would have come up then. But there was nothing in his stomach but the dryness of fear, just as the wetness of fear soaked his outer skin.

Now what? Kleenex, hairpins, all the little things a woman leaves scattered around the room. Yes, and her purse. It had some money in it, but he didn't even bother to look. He didn't want the money. He just wanted to get rid of everything — get rid of it fast, while luck still held.

He put the two bags in the car, on the front seat. Then he closed and locked the door of the room. Again he scanned the roadway in both directions. All clear.

Norman started the motor and switched on the lights. That was the dangerous part, using the lights. But he'd never be able to make it otherwise, not through the field. He drove slowly, up the slope behind the motel and along the gravel leading to the driveway and the house. Another stretch of gravel went to the rear of the house and terminated at the old shed which had been converted to serve as a garage for Norman's Chevy.

He shifted gears and eased off onto the grass. He was in the field now, bumping along. There was a rutted path here, worn by tire tracks, and he found it. Every few months Norman took his own car along this route, hitching up the trailer and going into the woods bordering the swamp to collect firewood for the kitchen.

That's what he'd do tomorrow, he decided. First thing in the morning, he'd take the car and trailer out there. Then his own tire marks would cover up these. And if he left footprints in the mud, there'd be an explanation.

If he *needed* an explanation, that is. But maybe his luck would hold.

It held long enough for him to reach the edge of the swamp and do what he had to do. Once back there he switched off the headlights and taillights and worked in the dark. It wasn't easy, and it took a long time, but he managed. Starting the motor and shifting into reverse, he jumped out and let it back down the slope into the muddy quagmire. The slope would show tire tracks too, and he must remember to smooth away the traces. But that wasn't the important thing now. Just as long as the car sank. He could see the muck bubbling and rising up over the wheels. God, it had to keep sinking now; if it didn't, he could never pull it out again. It *had* to sink! The fenders were going under, slowly, very slowly. How long had he been standing here? It seemed like hours, and still the car was visible. But the ooze had reached the door handles; it was coming up over the side-glass and the windshield. There wasn't a sound to be heard; the car kept descending, inch by silent inch. Now only the top was visible. Suddenly there was a sort of sucking noise, a nasty and abrupt *plop!* And the car was gone. It had settled beneath the surface of the swamp.

Norman didn't know how deep the swamp was at this point. He could only hope the car would keep on going down. Down, deep down, where nobody could ever find it.

He turned away with a grimace. Well, that part of it was finished. The car was in the swamp. And the hamper was in the trunk. And the body was in the hamper. The twisted torso and the bloody head —

But he couldn't think about *that*. He *mustn't*. There were other things to do.

He did them, did them almost mechanically. There was soap and detergent in the office, a brush and a pail. He went over the bathroom inch by inch, then the shower stall. As long as he concentrated on scrubbing, it wasn't so bad, even though the smell sickened him.

Then he inspected the bedroom once more. Luck was still with him; just under the bed he found an earring. He hadn't noticed that she was wearing earrings earlier in the evening, but she must have been. Maybe it had slipped off when she shook out her hair. If not, the other one would be around here somewhere. Norman was bleary-eyed and weary, but he searched. It wasn't anywhere in the room, so it must either be in her baggage or still attached to her ear. In either case, it wouldn't matter. Just as long as he got rid of this one. Throw it in the swamp tomorrow.

Now there was only the house to attend to. He'd scrub out the kitchen sink.

It was almost two o'clock by the grandfather clock in the hall when he came in. He could scarcely keep his eyes open long enough to wash the stains from the sink top. Then he stepped out of his muddy shoes, peeled off the coveralls, stripped himself of shirt and socks, and washed. The water was cold as ice but it didn't revive him. His body was numb.

Tomorrow morning he'd go back down into the swamp with his own car; he'd wear the same clothing again and it wouldn't matter if it showed mud and dirt. Just as long as there was no blood anywhere. No blood on his clothes, no blood on his body, no blood on his hands.

There. Now he was clean again. His hands were clean. He could move his numb legs, propel his numb body up the stairs and into the bedroom, sink into bed and sleep. With clean hands.

It wasn't until he was actually in the bedroom, donning his pajamas, that he remembered what was still wrong.

Mother hadn't come back.

She was still wandering around, God knows where, in the middle of the night. He had to get dressed again and go out, he had to find her.

Or — did he?

The thought came creeping, just as the numbness came creeping, stealing over his senses, softly, smoothly, there in the silken silence.

Why should *he* concern himself about Mother, after what she had done? Maybe she had been picked up, or would be. Maybe she'd even babble out the story of what she'd done. But who'd believe it? There was no evidence, not any more. All he'd need to do was deny everything. Maybe he wouldn't even have to do that much — anyone who saw Mother, listened to her wild story, would know she was crazy. And then they'd lock her up, lock her up in a place where she didn't have a key and couldn't get out again, and that would be the end.

He hadn't felt like that earlier this evening, he remembered. But that was before he had to go into that bathroom again, before he had to go into the shower stall and see those — *things*.

Mother had done that to him. Mother had done that to the poor, helpless girl. She had taken a butcher knife and she had hacked and ripped — nobody but a maniac could have committed such an atrocity. He had to face facts. She *was* a maniac. She *deserved* to be put away, *had* to be put away, for her own safety as well as the safety of others.

If they did pick her up, he'd see that it happened.

But the chances were, actually, that she wouldn't go anywhere near the highway. Most likely she had stayed right around the house, or the yard. Maybe she had even followed him down into the swamp; she could have been watching him all the time. Of course, if she were really out of her head, then anything might happen. If she *had* gone to the swamp, perhaps she'd slipped. It was quite possible, there in the dark. He remembered the way the car had gone down, disappearing in the quicksand.

Norman knew he wasn't thinking clearly any more. He was faintly aware of the fact that he was lying on the bed, had been lying on the bed for a long time now. And he wasn't really deciding what to do, either, or wondering about Mother and where she was. Instead, he was *watching* her. He could *see* her now, even though at the same time he felt the numb pressure on his eyeballs and knew that his eyelids were closed.

He could see Mother, and she *was* in the swamp. That's where she was, in the swamp, she'd blundered down the bank in the darkness and she couldn't get out again. The muck was bubbling up around her knees, she was trying to grab a branch or something solid and pull herself out again, but it was no use. Her hips were sinking under, her dress was pressed tight in a V across the front of her thighs. Mother's thighs were dirty. Mustn't look.

But he *wanted* to look, he *wanted* to see her go down, down into the soft, wet, slimy darkness. She deserved it, she deserved to go down, to join that poor, innocent girl. Good riddance! In a little while now he'd be free of them both — victim and victor, Mother and the bitch, bitch-Mother down there in the dirty slime, let it happen, let her drown in the filthy, nasty scum —

Now it was up over her breasts, he didn't like to think about such things, he never thought about Mother's breasts, he mustn't, and it was good that they were disappearing, sinking away forever, so he'd never think about such things again. But he could see her gasping for breath, and it made him gasp too; he felt as if he were choking with her and then (*it was a dream, it had to be a dream!*) Mother was suddenly standing on the firm ground at the edge of the swamp and *he* was sinking. *He* was in filth up to his neck and there was nobody to save him, nobody to help

73

him, nothing to hang onto unless Mother held out her arms. *She* could save him, she was the only one! He didn't want to drown, he didn't want to strangle and suffocate in the slime, he didn't want to go down there the way the girl-bitch had gone down. And now he remembered why she was there; it was because she had been killed, and she had been killed because she was evil. She had flaunted herself before him, she had deliberately tempted him with the perversion of her nakedness. Why, he'd wanted to kill her himself when she did that, because Mother had taught him about evil and the ways of evil and thou shalt not suffer a bitch to live.

So what Mother had done was to protect *him*, and he couldn't see her die, she wasn't wrong. He needed her now, and she needed him, and even if she was crazy she wouldn't let him go under now. She *couldn't*.

The foulness was sucking against his throat, it was kissing his lips and if he opened his mouth he knew he'd swallow it, but he had to open it to scream, and he *was* screaming. *'Mother, Mother — save me!'*

And then he was out of the swamp, back here in bed where he belonged, and his body was wet only with perspiration. He knew now that it had been a dream, even before he heard her voice there at the bedside.

'It's all right, son. I'm here. Everything's all right.' He could feel her hand on his forehead, and it was cool, like the drying sweat. He wanted to open his eyes, but she said, 'Don't you worry, son. Just go back to sleep.'

'But I have to tell you — '

'I know. I was watching. You didn't think I'd go away and leave you, did you? You did right, Norman. And everything's all right now.'

Yes. That was the way it should be. She was there to protect him. He was there to protect her. Just before he drifted off to sleep again, Norman made up his mind. They wouldn't talk about what had happened tonight — not now, or ever. And he wouldn't think about sending her away. No matter what she did, she belonged here, with him. Maybe she was crazy, and a murderess, but she was all he had. All he wanted. All he needed. Just knowing she was here, beside him, as he went to sleep.

Norman stirred, turned, and then fell into a darkness deeper and more engulfing than the swamp.

6

Promptly at six o'clock on the following Friday evening, a miracle happened.

Ottorino Respighi came into the back room of Fairvale's only hardware store to play his *Brazilian Impressions*.

Ottorino Respighi had been dead for many years, and the symphonic group — *l' Orchestre des Concertes Colonne* — had been conducted in the work many thousands of miles away.

But when Sam Loomis reached out and switched on the tiny FM radio, the music welled forth, annihilating space and time and death itself.

It was, as far as he understood it, an authentic miracle.

For a moment, Sam wished that he weren't alone. Miracles are meant to be shared. Music is meant to be shared. But there was no one in Fairvale who would recognize either the music itself or the miracle of its coming. Fairvale people were inclined to be practical about things. Music was just something you got when you put a nickel in a jukebox or turned on the television set.

Mostly it was rock-'n-roll, but once in a while there'd be some longhair stuff like that *William Tell* piece they played for westerns. What's so wonderful about this Ottorino What's-His-Name, or whoever he is?

Sam Loomis shrugged, then grinned. He wasn't complaining about the situation. Maybe small-town people didn't dig his sort of music, but at least they left him the freedom to enjoy it for himself. Just as he made no attempt to influence their tastes. It was a fair bargain.

Sam pulled out the big ledger and carried it over to the kitchen table. For the next hour, the table would double in brass as his desk. Just as he would double in brass as his own bookkeeper.

That was one of the drawbacks of living here in one room behind the hardware store. There was no extra space available, and everything doubled in brass. Still, he accepted the situation. It wouldn't go on this way very much longer, the way things were breaking for him these days.

A quick glance at the figures seemed to confirm his optimism. He'd have to do some checking on inventory requirements, but it looked very much as if he might be able to pay off another thousand this month. That would bring the total up to three thousand for the half-year mark. And this was off-season, too. There'd be more business coming in this fall.

Sam scribbled a hasty figure-check on a sheet of scratch paper. Yes, he could probably swing it. Made him feel pretty good. It ought to make Mary feel pretty good, too.

Mary hadn't been too cheerful, lately. At least her letters sounded as if she were depressed. When she wrote at all, that is. Come to think of it, she owed him several letters now. He'd written her again, last Friday, and still no reply. Maybe she was sick. No, if that was the case he'd have gotten a note from the kid sister, Lila, or whatever her name was. Chances were that Mary was just discouraged, down in the dumps. Well, he didn't blame her. She'd been sweating things out for a long time.

So had he, of course. It wasn't easy, living like this. But it was the only way. She understood, she agreed to wait.

Maybe he ought to take a few days off next week, leave Summerfield in charge here, and take a run down to see her. Just drop in and surprise her, cheer her up. Why not? Things were very slack at the moment, and Bob could handle the store alone.

Sam sighed. The music was descending now, spiraling to a minor key. This must be the theme for the snake garden. Yes, he recognized it, with its slithering strings, its writhing woodwinds squirming over the sluggish bass. Snakes. Mary didn't like snakes. Chances were, she didn't like this kind of music, either.

Sometimes he almost wondered if they hadn't made a mistake when they planned ahead. After all, what did they really know about each other? Aside from the companionship of the cruise and the two days Mary had spent here last year, they'd never been together. There were the letters, of course, but maybe they just made things worse. Because in the letters, Sam had begun to find another Mary — a moody, almost petulant personality, given to likes and dislikes so emphatic they were almost prejudices.

He shrugged. What had come over him? Was it the morbidity of the music? All at once he felt tension in the muscles at the back of his neck. He listened intently, trying to isolate the instrument, pinpoint the phrase that had triggered his reaction. Something was wrong, something he sensed, something he could almost hear.

Sam rose, pushing back his chair.

He could hear it now. A faint rattling, from up front. Of course, that's all it was; he had heard something to bother him. Somebody was turning the knob of the front door.

The store was closed for the night, the shades drawn, but maybe it was some tourist. Most likely would be; folks in town knew when he closed up, and they also knew he lived in the back room. If they wanted to come down for anything after regular hours, they'd phone first.

Well, business was business, whoever the customer might be. Sam turned and went into the store, hurrying down the dim aisle. The blind had been pulled down on the front door, but he could hear the agitated rattling very plainly now — in fact, some of the pots and pans on the traffic-item counter were jiggling.

This must be an emergency, all right; probably the customer needed a new bulb for his kid's Mickey Mouse flashlight.

Sam fumbled in his pocket, pulling out his key ring. 'All right,' he called. 'I'm opening up.' And did so, deftly, swinging the door back without withdrawing the key.

She stood there in the doorway, silhouetted against the street lamp's glow from the curbing outside. For a moment the shock of recognition held him immobile; then he stepped forward and his arms closed around her.

'Mary!' he murmured. His mouth found

hers, gratefully, greedily; and then she was stiffening, she was pulling away, her hands had come up shaping into balled fists that beat against his chest. What was wrong?

'I'm not Mary!' she gasped. 'I'm Lila.'

'Lila?' He stepped back once more. 'The kid — I mean, Mary's sister?'

She nodded. As she did so he caught a glimpse of her face in profile, and the lamplight glinted on her hair. It was brown, much lighter than Mary's. Now he could see the difference in the shape of the snub nose, the higher angle of the broad cheekbones. She was a trifle shorter, too, and her hips and shoulders seemed slimmer.

'I'm sorry,' he murmured. 'It's this light.'

'That's all right.' Her voice was different, too; softer and lower.

'Come inside, won't you?'

'Well — ' She hesitated, glancing down at her feet, and then Sam noticed the small suitcase on the sidewalk.

'Here, let me take this for you.' He scooped it up. As he passed her in the doorway he switched on the rear light. 'My room is in back,' he told her. 'Follow me.'

She trailed after him in silence. Not quite silence, because Respighi's tone poem still resounded from the radio. As they entered his makeshift living quarters, Sam went over to

81

switch it off. She lifted her hand.

'Don't,' she told him. 'I'm trying to recognize that music.' She nodded. 'Villa-Lobos?'

'Respighi. Something called *Brazilian Impressions*. It's on the Urania label, I believe.'

'Oh. We don't stock that.' For the first time he remembered that Lila worked in a record shop.

'You want me to leave it on, or do you want to talk?' he asked.

'Turn it off. We'd better talk.'

He nodded, bent over the set, then faced her. 'Sit down,' he invited. 'Take off your coat.'

'Thanks. I don't intend to stay long. I've got to find a room.'

'You're here on a visit?'

'Just overnight. I'll probably leave again in the morning. And it isn't exactly a visit. I'm looking for Mary.'

'Looking for — ' Sam stared at her. 'But what would she be doing here?'

'I was hoping you could tell me that.'

'But how could I? Mary isn't here.'

'*Was* she here? Earlier this week, I mean?'

'Of course not. Why, I haven't seen her since she drove up last summer.' Sam sat down on the sofa bed. 'What's the matter, Lila? What's this all about?'

'I wish I knew.'

She avoided his gaze, lowering her lashes and staring at her hands. They twisted in her lap, twisted like serpents. In the brighter light, Sam noticed that her hair was almost blonde. She didn't resemble Mary at all, now. She was quite another girl. A nervous, unhappy girl.

'Please,' he said. 'Tell me.'

Lila looked up suddenly, her wide hazel eyes searching his. 'You weren't lying when you said Mary hasn't been here?'

'No, it's the truth. I haven't even heard from her these last few weeks. I was beginning to get worried. Then you come bursting in here and — ' His voice broke. 'Tell me!'

'All right. I believe you. But there isn't much to tell.' She took a deep breath and started to speak again, her hands roaming restlessly across the front of her skirt. 'I haven't seen Mary since a week ago last night, at the apartment. That's the night I left for Dallas, to see some wholesale suppliers down there — I do the buying for the shop. Anyway, I spent the weekend and took a train back up late Sunday night. I got in early Monday morning. Mary wasn't at the apartment. At first I wasn't concerned; maybe she'd left early for work. But she usually called me sometime during the day, and when she didn't phone by noon, I decided to call her at the office. Mr. Lowery answered the phone. He said he was just getting ready to call me and see what was wrong. Mary hadn't come in that morning. He hadn't seen or heard from her since the middle of Friday afternoon.'

'Wait a minute,' Sam said, slowly. 'Let me get this straight. Are you trying to tell me that Mary has been missing for an entire week?'

'I'm afraid so.'

'Then why wasn't I notified before this?' He stood up, feeling the renewed tension in his neck muscles, feeling it in his throat and his voice. 'Why didn't you get in touch with me, phone me? What about the police?'

'Sam, I — '

'Instead, you waited all this time and then came up here to ask if I'd seen her. It doesn't make sense!'

'Nothing makes sense. You see, the police don't know about this. And Mr. Lowery doesn't know about *you*. After what he told me, I agreed not to call them. But I was so worried, so frightened, and I had to know. That's why, today, I decided to drive up here and find out for myself. I thought maybe the two of you might have planned it together.'

'Planned what?' Sam shouted.

'That's what I'd like to know.' The answer was soft, but there was nothing soft about the face of the man who stood in the doorway. He was tall, thin, and deeply tanned; a gray Stetson shadowed his forehead but not his eyes. The eyes were ice-blue and ice-hard.

'Who are you?' Sam muttered. 'How did you get in here?'

'Front door was unlocked, so I just stepped inside. I came here to get a little information, but I see Miss Crane already beat me to the question. Maybe you'd like to give us both an answer now.'

'Answer?'

'That's right.' The tall man moved forward, one hand dipping into the pocket of his gray jacket. Sam lifted his arm, then dropped it, as the hand came forth, extending a wallet. The tall man flipped it open. 'The name's Arbogast. Milton Arbogast. Licensed investigator, representing Parity Mutual. We carry a bonding policy on the Lowery Agency your girl-friend worked for. That's why I'm here now. I want to find out what you two did with the forty thousand dollars.'

7

The gray Stetson was on the table now, and the gray jacket was draped over the back of one of Sam's chairs. Arbogast snubbed his third cigarette in the ash tray and immediately lighted another.

'All right,' he said. 'So you didn't leave Fairvale any time during the past week. I'll buy that, Loomis. You'd know better than to lie. Too easy for me to check your story around town here.' The investigator inhaled slowly. 'Of course, that doesn't prove Mary Crane hasn't been to see *you*. She could have sneaked in some evening after your store closed, just like her sister did, tonight.'

Sam sighed. 'But she didn't. Look, you heard what Lila here just told you. I haven't even heard from Mary for weeks. I wrote her a letter last Friday, the very day she's supposed to have disappeared. Why would I do a thing like that if I knew she was going to come here?'

'To cover up, of course. Very smart move.' Arbogast exhaled savagely.

Sam rubbed the back of his neck. 'I'm not that smart. Not that smart at all. I didn't

86

know about the money. The way you've explained it, not even Mr. Lowery knew in advance that somebody was going to bring him forty thousand dollars in cash on Friday afternoon. Certainly Mary didn't know. How could we possibly plan anything together?'

'She could have phoned you from a pay station *after* she took the money, on Friday night, and told you to write her.'

'Check with the phone company here,' Sam answered wearily. 'You'll find I haven't had any long-distance calls for a month.'

Arbogast nodded. 'So she didn't phone you. She drove straight up, told you what had happened, and made a date to meet you later, after things cooled down.'

Lila bit her lip. 'My sister's not a criminal. You don't have any right to talk about her that way. You have no real proof that she took the money. Maybe Mr. Lowery took it himself. Maybe he cooked up this whole story, just to cover up — '

'Sorry,' Arbogast murmured. 'I know how you feel, but you can't make him your patsy. Unless the thief is found, tried and convicted, our company doesn't pay off — and Lowery is out the forty grand. So he couldn't profit from the deal in any way. Besides, you're overlooking obvious facts. Mary Crane is missing. She has been missing ever since the

87

afternoon she received that money. She didn't take it to the bank. She didn't hide it in the apartment. But it's gone. And her car is gone. And she's gone.' Again a cigarette died and was interred in the ash tray. 'It all adds up.'

Lila began to sob softly. 'No, it doesn't! You should have listened to me when I wanted to call the police. Instead I let you and Mr. Lowery talk me out of it. Because you said you wanted to keep things quiet, and maybe if we waited Mary would decide to bring the money back. You wouldn't believe what I said, but I know now that I was right. Mary didn't take that money. Somebody must have kidnapped her. Somebody who knew about it — '

Arbogast shrugged, then rose wearily and walked over to the girl. He patted her shoulder. 'Listen, Miss Crane — we went through this before, remember? Nobody else knew about the money. Your sister wasn't kidnapped. She went home and packed her own bags, drove off in her own car, and she was alone. Didn't your landlady see her go off? So be reasonable.'

'I *am* reasonable! You're the one who doesn't make sense! Following me up here to see Mr. Loomis — '

The investigator shook his head. 'What

makes you think I followed you?' he asked quietly.

'How else did you happen to come here tonight? You didn't know that Mary and Sam Loomis were engaged. Outside of me, no one knew. You didn't even know Sam Loomis existed.'

Arbogast shook his head. 'I knew. Remember, up at your apartment, when I looked through your sister's desk? I came across this envelope.' He flourished it.

'Why, it's addressed to me,' Sam muttered — and rose to reach for it.

Arbogast drew his hand away. 'You won't need this,' he said. 'There's no letter inside, just the envelope. But I can use it, because it's in her handwriting.' He paused. 'As a matter of fact, I *have* been using it, ever since Wednesday morning when I started out for here.'

'You started out for here — on *Wednesday?*' Lila dabbed at her eyes with a handkerchief.

'That's right. I wasn't following you. I was way ahead of you. The address on the envelope gave me a lead. That, plus Loomis' picture in the frame next to your sister's bed. *'With all my love — Sam.'* Easy enough to figure out the connection. So I decided to put myself in your sister's place. I've just laid my hands on forty thousand dollars in cash. I've got to get out of town, fast. Where do I go? Canada, Mexico, the West Indies? Too risky. Besides, I haven't had time to make long-range plans. My natural impulse would be to come straight to lover-boy, here.'

Sam hit the kitchen table so hard that the cigarette butts jumped out of the ash tray. 'That's about enough!' he said. 'You have no official right to make such accusations. So far you haven't offered one word of proof to back up any of this.'

Arbogast fumbled for another cigarette. 'You want proof, eh? What do you think I've been doing back there on the road, ever since Wednesday morning? That's when I found the car.'

'You found my sister's car?' Lila was on her feet.

'Sure. I had a funny hunch that one of the first things she'd do would be to ditch it. So I called around town, to all the dealers and the used car lots, giving a description and the license number. Sure enough, it paid off. I found the place. Showed the guy my credentials and he talked. Talked fast, too — guess he thought the car was hot. I didn't exactly contradict his notion, either.

'Turned out that Mary Crane made a fast trade with him on Friday night, just before

90

closing time. Took a hell of a beating on the deal, too. But I got all the info on the title, and a full description of the heap she drove out with. Heading north.

'So I headed north, too. But I couldn't go very fast. I was playing one hunch — that she'd stick to the highway because she was coming here. Probably drive straight through, the first night. So I drove straight through, for eight hours. Then I spent a lot of time around Oklahoma City, checking motels along the highway, and used car places on the road. I figured she might switch again, just to be on the safe side. But no dice. Thursday I got up as far as Tulsa. Same routine, same results. It wasn't until this morning when the needle turned up in the haystack. Another lot, another dealer, just north of there. She made the second trade early last Saturday — took another shellacking and ended up with a blue 1953 Plymouth, with a bad front fender.'

He took a notebook from his pocket. 'It's all down here in black and white,' he said. 'Title dope, engine number, everything. Both dealers are having photostats made and sending them back to the home office for me. But that doesn't matter, now. What matters is that Mary Crane drove north out of Tulsa on the main highway last Saturday morning, after switching cars twice in sixteen hours. As far as I'm concerned, this is the place she was heading for. And unless something unexpected happened — unless the car broke down, or there was an accident — she should have arrived here late last Saturday night.'

'But she didn't,' Sam said. 'I haven't seen her. Look, I can dig up proof, if you want it. Last Saturday night I was over at the Legion Hall, playing cards. Plenty of witnesses. Sunday morning I went to church. Sunday noon I had dinner at — '

Arbogast raised a hand wearily. 'Okay, I get the message. You didn't see her. So something must have happened. I'll start checking back.'

'What about the police?' Lila asked. 'I still think you ought to go to the police.' She moistened her lips. 'Suppose there *was* an accident — you couldn't stop at every hospital between here and Tulsa. Why, for all we know, Mary may be lying unconscious somewhere right now. She might even be — '

This time it was Sam who patted her shoulder. 'Nonsense,' he muttered. 'If anything like that had happened, you'd have been notified by now. Mary's all right.' But he glared over Lila's shoulder at the investigator. 'You can't do a thorough job all alone,' he said. 'Lila's being sensible. Why not let the police in on it? Report Mary missing, see if they can locate her.'

Arbogast picked up the gray Stetson. 'We've tried it the hard way so far. I admit it. Because if we could locate her without dragging in the authorities, we might save our client and the company a lot of bad publicity. For that matter, we could save Mary Crane some grief, too, if we picked her up ourselves and recovered the money. Maybe there wouldn't even be any charges that way. You've got to agree it was worth a try.'

'But if you're right, and Mary did get this far, then why hasn't she been to see me? That's what I want to know, just as badly as you do,' Sam told him. 'And I'm not going to wait much longer to find out.'

'Will you wait another twenty-four hours?' Arbogast asked.

'What do you have in mind?'

'More checking, like I said.' He raised his hand to forestall Sam's objections. 'Not all the way back to Tulsa — I admit that's impossible. But I'd like to nose around this territory a bit; visit the highway restaurants, filling stations, car dealers, motels. Maybe somebody saw her. Because I still think my hunch is right. She intended to come here. Perhaps she changed her mind after she arrived, and went on. But I'd like to be sure.'

'And if you don't find out in twenty-four hours — ?'

'Then I'm willing to call it quits, go to the police, do the whole Missing Persons routine. Okay?'

Sam glanced at Lila. 'What do you think?' he asked.

'I don't know. I'm so worried now, I *can't* think.' She sighed. 'Sam, you decide.'

He nodded at Arbogast. 'All right. It's a deal. But I'm warning you right now. If nothing happens tomorrow, and you don't notify the police, I will.'

Arbogast put on his jacket. 'Guess I'll get a room over at the hotel. How about you, Miss Crane?'

Lila looked at Sam. 'I'll take her over in a little while,' Sam said. 'First I thought we'd go and eat. But I'll see that she's checked in. And we'll both be here tomorrow. Waiting.'

For the first time that evening, Arbogast smiled. It wasn't the kind of a smile that would ever offer any competition to Mona Lisa, but it was a smile.

'I believe you,' he said. 'Sorry about the pressure act, but I had to make sure.' He nodded at Lila. 'We're going to find your sister for you. Don't you worry.'

Then he went out. Long before the front door closed behind him, Lila was sobbing

94

against Sam's shoulder. Her voice was a muffled moan. 'Sam, I'm scared — something's happened to Mary, I know it!'

'It's all right,' he said, wondering at the same time why there were no better words, why there never are any better words to answer fear and grief and loneliness. 'It's all right, believe me.'

Suddenly she stepped away from him, stepped back, and her tear-stained eyes went wide. Her voice, when it came, was low but firm.

'Why should I believe you, Sam?' she asked softly. 'Is there a reason? A reason you didn't tell that inspector? Sam — *was* Mary here to see you? Did you know about this, about the money?'

He shook his head. 'No, I didn't know. You'll have to take my word for that. The way I have to take yours.'

She turned away, facing the wall. 'I guess you're right,' she told him. 'Mary *could* have come to either one of us during the week, couldn't she? But she didn't. I trust you, Sam. Only it's just that it's so hard to believe anything any more, when your own sister turns out to be a — '

'Take it easy,' Sam cut in. 'What you need right now is a little food and a lot of rest. Things won't look so black tomorrow.'

'Do you *really* think so, Sam?'

'Yes, I do.'

It was the first time he'd ever lied to a woman.

8

Tomorrow became today, Saturday, and for Sam it was a time of waiting.

He phoned Lila from the store around ten, and she was already up, had already eaten breakfast. Arbogast wasn't in — apparently he'd gotten an early start. But he had left a note for Lila downstairs, saying that he would call in sometime during the day.

'Why don't you come over here and keep me company?' Sam suggested, over the phone. 'No sense sitting around in your room. We can have lunch together and check back at the hotel to see if Arbogast calls. Better still, I'll ask the operator to transfer any calls over here to the store.'

Lila agreed, and Sam felt better. He didn't want her to be alone today. Too easy for her to start brooding about Mary. God knows, he'd done enough of it himself, all night.

He'd done his best to resist the idea, but he had to admit that Arbogast's theory made sense. Mary must have planned to come here after she took the money. If she had taken it, that is.

That was the worst part: accepting Mary in

97

the role of a thief. Mary wasn't that kind of a person; everything he knew about her contradicted the possibility.

And yet, just how much did he know about Mary, really? Just last night he'd acknowledged to himself how little he actually understood his fiancée. Why, he knew so little that he'd even mistaken another girl for her, in a dim light.

Funny, Sam told himself, how we take it for granted that we know all there is to know about another person, just because we see them frequently or because of some strong emotional tie. Why, right here in Fairvale there were plenty of examples of what he meant. Like old Tomkins, superintendent of schools for years and a big wheel in Rotary, running away from his wife and family with a sixteen-year-old girl. Who ever suspected he'd do a thing like that? Any more than they'd suspected Mike Fisher, the biggest lush and gambler in this part of the state, would die and leave all his money to the Presbyterian Orphans' Home. Bob Summerfield, Sam's clerk in the store, had worked here every day for over a year before Sam knew he'd pulled a Section Eight in service — and for trying to beat out his chaplain's brains with a pistol butt, too. Bob was all right now, of course; a nicer, quieter guy you wouldn't find in a hundred years. But he'd been nice and quiet in the army, too, until something set him off. And nobody had noticed. Nice old ladies did away with their husbands after twenty years of happy marriage, meek little bank clerks suddenly up and embezzled the funds — you never could tell what might happen.

So perhaps Mary did steal the money. Perhaps she was tired of waiting for him to pay off his debts, and the sudden temptation was just too much. Maybe she thought she'd bring it here, cook up some story, get him to accept it. Maybe she planned for them to run away together. He had to be honest about the possibility, even the probability, that this was the case.

And if he granted that much, then he had to face the next question. Why hadn't she arrived? Where else could she have headed for after leaving the outskirts of Tulsa?

Once you began speculating about that, once you admitted to yourself that you didn't really know how another person's mind operated, then you came up against the ultimate admission — anything was possible. A decision to take a wild fling out in Las Vegas; a sudden impulse to drop out of sight completely and start a whole new life under another name; a traumatic excess of guilt, resulting in amnesia —

But he was beginning to make a federal case out of it, Sam told himself wryly. Or a clinical case. If he was going off on such farfetched speculations, he'd have to admit a thousand and one other alternatives. That she had been in an accident, as Lila feared, or picked up some hitchhiker who —

Again, Sam closed off the thought. He couldn't afford to carry it any further. It was bad enough keeping it to himself without the added burden of keeping it from Lila. His job today was to cheer her up. There was always the slim chance that Arbogast would find a lead. If not, he'd go to the authorities. Then, and only then, would he allow himself to think about the worst that might happen.

Talk about not knowing other people — why, when you came right down to it, you didn't even know yourself! He'd never suspected that he could entertain such sudden doubt and disloyalty concerning Mary. And yet how easily he'd slipped into accepting the attitude! It was unfair to her. The least he could do, in partial atonement, was to keep his suspicions from her sister.

Unless, of course, she was thinking the same things . . .

But Lila seemed in better spirits this morning. She'd changed into a lightweight suit, and when she came into the store her step was buoyant.

Sam introduced her to Bob Summerfield, then took her out to lunch. Inevitably, she began speculating about Mary and about what Arbogast might be doing today. Sam answered her briefly, attempting to keep both his replies and his tone of voice on a casual level. After their meal, he stopped at the hotel and arranged to have a transfer made on any calls which might come in for Lila during the afternoon.

Then they went back to the store. It was a light day, for Saturday, and much of the time Sam was able to sit in the back room and chat with the girl. Summerfield handled the customers, and it was only occasionally that Sam had to excuse himself and step out to take care of matters.

Lila seemed relaxed and at ease. She switched on the radio, picked up a symphonic program on AM, and listened with apparent absorption. Sam found her sitting there when he returned from one of his trips up front.

'Bartok's *Concerto for Orchestra*, isn't it?' he asked.

She looked up, smiling. 'That's right. Funny, your knowing so much about music.'

'What's so strange about that? This is the age of hi-fi, remember? Just because a person lives in a small town doesn't mean he can't be interested in music, books, art. And I've had a lot of time to fill.'

Lila smoothed the collar of her blouse. 'Maybe I've got things backwards, then. Maybe the funny thing isn't that you're interested in things like this, but that you're also in the hardware business. The two just don't seem to go together.'

'There's nothing wrong with the hardware business.'

'I didn't mean to imply that. But it seems, well, so — trivial.'

Sam sat down at the table. Suddenly he stooped and picked up an object from the floor. It was small, pointed, and shiny.

'Trivial,' he echoed. 'Perhaps. Then again, maybe it's all in the way you look at it. For example, what's this in my hand?'

'A nail, isn't it?'

'That's right. Just a nail. I sell them by the pound. Hundreds of pounds a year. Dad used to sell them too. I'll bet we've probably sold ten tons of nails out of this store alone since it opened for business. All lengths, all sizes, just common ordinary nails. But there's nothing trivial about a single one of them. Not when you stop to think about it.

'Because every nail serves a purpose. An important, a lasting purpose. You know something? Maybe half the frame houses here in Fairvale are held together by nails we've sold right here. I guess it's a little silly of me, but sometimes when I walk down the street here in town I get the feeling that I helped build it. The tools I sold shaped the boards and finished them. I've provided the paint that covers the houses, the brushes which applied it, the storm doors and screens, the glass for the windows — ' He broke off, with a self-conscious grin. 'Listen to the Master Builder, will you? But no, I mean it. Everything in this business makes sense, because it serves a real purpose, fills a need that's a part of living. Even a single nail, like this one, fulfills a function. Drive it into a crucial place and you can depend on it to do a job, keep on doing it for a hundred years to come. Long after we're dead and gone, both of us.'

The moment he said the words he regretted them. But it was too late now. He watched the smile fade from her lips, as if on cue.

'Sam, I'm worried. It's almost four now, and Arbogast hasn't called — '

'He will. Just be patient; give him time.'

'I can't help it! You said twenty-four hours, and then you'd go to the police if you had to.'

'I meant it. But it won't be twenty-four

hours until eight o'clock. And I still say maybe we won't have to go. Maybe Arbogast is right.'

'Maybe! Sam, I want to *know!*' She smoothed her blouse again, but her brow remained wrinkled. 'You aren't fooling me for one minute, with all this routine about nails. You're just as nervous as I am. Aren't you?'

'Yes. I guess so.' He stood up, swinging his arms. 'I don't know why Arbogast hasn't called in by now. There aren't that many places in this area to check, not if he stopped at every highway hamburger joint and motel in the county! If he doesn't get in touch with us by supper-time, I'll go over to Jud Chambers myself.'

'Who?'

'Jud Chambers. He's the sheriff here. Fairvale's the county seat, you know.'

'Sam, I — '

The phone rang, out in the store. He disappeared without waiting for her to complete her sentence. Bob Summerfield was already answering.

'It's for you,' he called.

Sam picked up the receiver, glancing over his shoulder and noting that Lila had followed him out.

'Hello — Sam Loomis speaking.'

104

'Arbogast. Thought you might be worried about me.'

'We were. Lila and I have been sitting here and waiting for you to call. What did you find out?'

There was a short, almost imperceptible pause. Then, 'No dice, so far.'

'So far? Where have you been all day?'

'Where haven't I been? I've covered this area from one end to another. Right now I'm in Parnassus.'

'That's way down at the edge of the county, isn't it? What about the highway between?'

'I came out on it. But I understand I can come back another way, on an alternate.'

'Yes, that's right. The old highway — it's a county trunk now. But there's absolutely nothing along that route. Not even a filling station.'

'Fellow in the restaurant here tells me there's a motel back in through there.'

'Oh — come to think of it, I guess there is. The old Bates place. I didn't know it was still open. It isn't likely you'll find anything there.'

'Well, it's the last on the list. I'm coming back anyway, so I might as well stop in. How you holding?'

'All right.'

'And the girl?'

Sam lowered his voice. 'She wants me to notify the authorities immediately. And I think she's right. After what you've told me, I know she's right.'

'Will you wait until I get there?'

'How long is it going to take?'

'An hour, maybe. Unless I run into something at this motel.' Arbogast hesitated. 'Look, we made a bargain. I'm willing to keep my end of it. All I'm asking is for you to wait until I come back to town. Let me go with you to the police. It'll be a lot easier to get co-operation that way, with me along. You know how it is with small-town law. The minute you ask them to put through a long-distance call they press the panic button.'

'We'll give you an hour,' Sam said. 'You can find us here at the store.'

He hung up and turned away.

'What did he say?' Lila asked. 'He didn't find out anything, did he?'

'Well, no, but he isn't finished yet. There's another place where he plans to stop — '

'Only one more place?'

'Don't say it like that. Maybe he'll hear something there. If not, he's due back within an hour. We'll go to the sheriff. You heard what I told him.'

'All right. We'll wait. One hour, you said.'

It wasn't a pleasant hour. Sam was almost grateful when the late Saturday afternoon crowd came in and he had an excuse to go out front and help wait on the overflow. He couldn't pretend to be cheerful any longer, couldn't make small talk. Not to her, nor to himself.

Because he was beginning to feel it now.

Something had happened.

Something had happened to Mary.

Something —

'Sam!'

He turned away from the cash register after completing a sale, and Lila was there. She'd come out from the back room and she was pointing at her wrist watch. 'Sam, the hour's up!'

'I know. Let's give him a few more minutes, shall we? I've got to close up the store first, anyway.'

'All right. But only a few minutes. *Please!* If you knew how I felt — '

'I do know.' He squeezed her arm, squeezed out a smile. 'Don't worry, he'll be here any second.'

But he didn't come.

Sam and Summerfield shooed out the last straggler at five-thirty. Sam checked the register and Summerfield spread the dust covers for the night.

Still Arbogast didn't appear.

Summerfield switched off the lights, prepared to depart. Sam got ready to lock the door.

No Arbogast.

'Now,' Lila said. 'Let's go now. If you don't, then I w — '

'Listen!' Sam said. 'It's the phone.'

And, seconds later, 'Hello?'

'Arbogast.'

'Where are you? You promised to — '

'Never mind what I promised.' The investigator's voice was low, his words hurried. 'I'm out at the motel, and I've only got a minute. Wanted to let you know why I hadn't showed. Listen, I've found a lead. Your girl-friend was here, all right. Last Saturday night.'

'Mary? You're sure?'

'Pretty sure. I checked the register, got a chance to compare handwriting. Of course she used another name — Jane Wilson — and gave a phony address. I'll have to get a court order to photostat the register entry, if we need proof.'

'What else did you find out?'

'Well, the car description tallies, and so does the description of the girl. The proprietor filled me in.'

'How'd you manage to get that information?'

108

'I pulled my badge and gave him the stolen car routine. He got all excited. A real oddball, this guy. Name's Norman Bates. You know him?'

'No, can't say that I do.'

'He says the girl drove in Saturday night, around six. Paid in advance. It was a bad night, raining, and she was the only customer. Claims she pulled out early the next morning, before he came down to open up. He lives in a house behind the motel with his mother.'

'Do you think he's telling the truth?'

'I don't know, yet.'

'What does that mean?'

'Well, I put a little heat on him, about the car and all. And he let it slip that he'd invited the girl up to the house for supper. Said that was all there was to it, his mother could verify it.'

'Did you talk to her?'

'No, but I'm going to. She's up at the house, in her room. He tried to hand me a line that she's too sick to see anyone, but I noticed her sitting at the bedroom window giving me the once-over when I drove in. So I told him I was going to have a little chat with his old lady whether he liked it or not.'

'But you have no authority — '

'Look, you want to find out about your girl-friend, don't you? And he doesn't seem to know anything about search warrants. Anyway, he hotfooted it off to the house, to tell his mother to get dressed. I thought I'd sneak through a call while he's gone. So you stick around until I'm finished here. Oh-oh, he's coming back. See you.'

The receiver clicked and the line went dead. Sam hung up. He turned to Lila and reported the conversation.

'Feel better, now?'

'Yes. But I wish I knew — '

'We will know, in just a little while. Now all we have to do is wait.'

9

Saturday afternoon, Norman shaved. He shaved only once a week, and always on a Saturday.

Norman didn't like to shave, because of the mirror. It had those wavy lines in it. All mirrors seemed to have wavy lines that hurt his eyes.

Maybe the real trouble was that his eyes were bad. Yes, that was it, because he remembered how he used to enjoy looking in the mirror as a boy. He liked to stand in front of the glass without any clothes on. One time Mother caught him at it and hit him on the side of the head with the big silver-handled hairbrush. She hit him hard, and it hurt. Mother said that was a nasty thing to do, to look at yourself that way.

He could still remember how it hurt, and how his head ached afterward. From then on it seemed he got a headache almost every time he looked in a mirror. Mother finally took him to the doctor and the doctor said he needed glasses. The glasses helped, but he still had trouble seeing properly when he gazed into a mirror. So after a while, he just didn't, except when he couldn't help it. And Mother was right. It *was* nasty to stare at yourself, all naked and unprotected; to peek at the blubbery fat, the short hairless arms, the big belly, and underneath it —

When you did, you wished you were somebody else. Somebody who was tall and lean and handsome, like Uncle Joe Considine. 'Isn't he the best-looking figure of a man you ever saw?' Mother used to remark.

It was the truth, too, and Norman had to admit it. But he still hated Uncle Joe Considine, even if he *was* handsome. And he wished Mother wouldn't insist on calling him 'Uncle Joe.' Because he wasn't any real relation at all — just a friend who came around to visit Mother. And he got her to build the motel, too, after she sold the farm acreage.

That was strange. Mother always talked against men, and about Your-father-who-ran-off-and-deserted-me, and yet Uncle Joe Considine could wrap her around his little finger. He could do anything he wanted with Mother. It would be nice to be like that, and to look the way Uncle Joe Considine looked.

Oh, no, it wouldn't! Because Uncle Joe was dead.

Norman blinked at his reflection as he shaved. Funny how it had slipped his mind.

Why it must be almost twenty years now. Time is relative, of course. Einstein said so, and he wasn't the first to discover it — the ancients knew it too, and so did some of the modern mystics like Aleister Crowley and Ouspensky. Norman had read them all, and he even owned some of the books. Mother didn't approve; she claimed these things were against religion, but that wasn't the real reason. It was because when he read the books he wasn't her little boy any more. He was a grown man, a man who studied the secrets of time and space and mastered the secrets of dimension and being.

It was like being two people, really — the child and the adult. Whenever he thought about Mother, he became a child again, with a child's vocabulary, frames of reference, and emotional reactions. But when he was by himself — not actually by himself, but off in a book — he was a mature individual. Mature enough to understand that he might even be the victim of a mild form of schizophrenia, most likely some form of borderline neurosis.

Granted, it wasn't the healthiest situation in the world. Being Mother's little boy had its drawbacks. On the other hand, as long as he recognized the dangers he could cope with them, and with Mother. It was just lucky for her that he knew when to be a man; that he *did* know a few things about psychology and parapsychology too.

It had been lucky when Uncle Joe Considine died, and it was lucky again last week, when that girl came along. If he hadn't acted as an adult, Mother would be in real trouble right now.

Norman fingered the razor. It was sharp, very sharp. He had to be careful not to cut himself. Yes, and he had to be careful to put it away when he finished shaving, to lock it up where Mother couldn't get hold of it. He couldn't trust Mother with anything that sharp. That's why he did most of the cooking, and the dishes too. Mother still loved to clean house — her own room was always neat as a pin — but Norman always took charge of the kitchen. Not that he ever said anything to her, outright; he just took over.

She never questioned him, either, and he was glad of that. Things had gone along for a whole week now, since that girl had come last Saturday, and they hadn't discussed the affair at all. It would have been awkward and embarrassing for both of them; Mother must have sensed it, for it seemed as if she deliberately avoided him — she spent a lot of time just resting in her room, and didn't have much to say. Probably her conscience bothered her.

And that was as it should be. Murder was a terrible thing. Even if you're not quite right in the head, you can realize that much. Mother must be suffering quite a bit.

Perhaps catharsis would help her, but Norman was glad she hadn't spoken. Because *he* was suffering too. It wasn't conscience that plagued him — it was fear.

All week long he'd waited for something to go wrong. Every time a car drove into the motel driveway, he just about jumped out of his skin. Even when cars merely drove past on the old highway, it made him nervous.

Last Sunday, of course, he'd finished cleaning up back there at the edge of the swamp. He took his own car down there and loaded the trailer with wood, and by the time he'd finished there wasn't anything left that would look suspicious. The girl's earring had gone into the swamp, too. And the other one hadn't shown up. So he felt reasonably secure.

But on Thursday night, when the State Highway Patrol car pulled into the driveway, he almost passed out. The officer just wanted to use the phone. Afterward, Norman was able to laugh at himself, yet at the time it wasn't a joke to him at all.

Mother had been sitting at her window in the bedroom, and it was just as well the

115

officer hadn't seen her. Mother had looked out of the window a lot during the past week. Maybe she was worried about visitors too. Norman tried to tell her to stay out of sight, but he couldn't bring himself to explain why. Any more than he could discuss with her why he wouldn't permit her to come down to the motel and help out. He just saw to it that she didn't. The house was the place where she belonged — you couldn't trust Mother around strangers, not any more. And the less they knew about her, the better. He should never have told that girl —

Norman finished shaving and washed his hands again. He'd noticed this compulsion in himself, particularly during the past week. Guilt feelings. A regular Lady Macbeth. Shakespeare had known a lot about psychology. Norman wondered if he had known other things too. There was the ghost of Hamlet's father, for example.

No time to think about that now. He had to get down to the motel and open up.

There'd been some business during the week, not very much. Norman never had more than three or four units occupied on a given night, and that was good. It meant he didn't need to rent out Number Six. Number Six had been the girl's room.

He hoped he'd never have to rent it out.

He was done with that sort of thing — the peeking, the voyeurism. That was what caused all the trouble in the first place. If he hadn't peeked, if he hadn't been drinking —

No sense crying over spilt milk, though. Even if it hadn't been *milk*.

Norman wiped his hands, turning away from the mirror. Forget the past, let the dead bury the dead. Things were working out fine, and that was the only thing he had to remember. Mother was behaving herself, he was behaving himself, they were together as they always had been. A whole week had gone by without any trouble, and there wouldn't *be* any trouble from now on. Particularly if he held firm to his resolve to behave like an adult instead of a child, a Mamma's Boy. And he'd already made up his mind about *that*.

He tightened his tie and left the bathroom. Mother was in her room, looking out of the window again. Norman wondered if he ought to say anything to her. No, better not. There might be an argument, and he wasn't quite ready yet to face her. Let her look if she liked. Poor, sick old lady, chained to the house here. Let her watch the world go by.

That was the child speaking, of course. But he was willing to make such a concession, as long as he behaved like a sensible adult. As long as he locked the downstairs doors when he went out.

It was locking the doors all week long which gave him his new sense of security. He'd taken her keys away from her, too — the keys to the house and the keys to the motel. Once he left, there was no way she could get out. She was safe in the house and he was safe in the motel. There could be no repetition of what had happened last week as long as he observed the precaution. After all, it was for her own good. Better the house than an asylum.

Norman walked down the path and came around the corner toward his office just as the towel-service truck drove up on its weekly rounds. He had everything ready for the driver. He accepted the fresh supply and gave him the old, dirty linen. The towel service handled the laundering of sheets and pillowcases, too. That made it simple. Actually, there was no trick to operating a motel these days.

After the truck departed Norman went in and cleaned up Number Four — some traveling salesman from up in Illinois had pulled out earlier in the day. Left the usual mess, too. Cigarette butts on the edge of the washbowl, and a magazine on the floor next to the toilet seat. One of those science fiction things. Norman chuckled as he picked it up. Science fiction! If they only *knew!*

But they didn't know. They'd never know, and they must not know. As long as he was careful about Mother, there'd be no risk. He had to protect her, and he had to protect others. What had happened last week proved it. From now on he'd be extra careful, always. For everyone's sake.

Norman walked back to the office and put the towels away. There was already a fresh supply of linen in every unit. He was ready for today's business — if any.

But nothing happened until around four o'clock. He sat there watching the roadway outside, and he got bored and fidgety. He was almost tempted to take a drink, until he remembered what he'd promised himself. No more drinking. That was part of the trouble, when there was trouble. He couldn't afford to drink, not even a drop. Drinking had killed Uncle Joe Considine. Drinking had led to the killing of the girl, indirectly. So from now on he'd be a teetotaler. Still, he could use a drink right now. Just one —

Norman was still hesitating when the car pulled in. Alabama plates. A middle-aged couple climbed out and came into the office. The man was bald and wore heavy, dark-rimmed glasses. The woman was fat and perspiring. Norman showed them Number One, way at the other end, for ten dollars, double. The woman complained about the stuffiness in a high, whining drawl, but she seemed satisfied when Norman switched on the fan. The man took their bags, and signed the register. *Mr. and Mrs. Herman Pritzler, Birmingham, Ala.* They were just tourists; they wouldn't present any problems.

Norman sat down again, riffling the pages of the science fiction magazine he'd found. The light was dim; must be around five o'clock now. He switched on the lamp.

Another car rolled up the drive, with a lone man behind the wheel. Probably another salesman. Green Buick, Texas license.

Texas license! That girl, that Jane Wilson, had come from Texas!

Norman stood up and stepped behind the counter. He saw the man leave the car, heard the crunch of his approaching footsteps on the gravel, matched the rhythm with the muffled thumping of his own heart.

It's just coincidence, he told himself. *People drive up from Texas every day. Why, Alabama is even further away.*

The man entered. He was tall and thin, and he wore one of those gray Stetson hats with a broad brim that shadowed the upper portion of his face. His chin showed tan under the heavy stubble of beard.

'Good evening,' he said, without much of a drawl.

'Good evening.' Norman shifted his feet uneasily underneath the counter.

'You the proprietor here?'

'That's right. Would you like a room?'

'Not exactly. I'm looking for a little information.'

'I'll be glad to help, if I can. What is it you wanted to know?'

'I'm trying to locate a girl.'

Norman's hands twitched. He couldn't feel them, because they were numb. He was numb all over. His heart wasn't pounding any more — it didn't even seem to be beating. Everything was very quiet. It would be terrible if he screamed.

'Her name is Crane,' the man said. 'Mary Crane. From Fort Worth, Texas. I was wondering if she might have registered here.'

Norman didn't want to scream now. He wanted to laugh. He could feel his heart resume its normal functions again. It was easy to reply.

'No,' he said, 'There hasn't been anybody by that name here.'

'You sure?'

'Positive. We don't get too much business

these days. I'm pretty good at remembering my customers.'

'This girl would have stopped over about a week ago. Last Saturday night, say, or Sunday.'

'I didn't have anyone here over the weekend. Weather was bad in these parts.'

'Are you sure? This girl — woman, I should say — is about twenty-seven. Five feet five, weight around one-twenty, dark hair, blue eyes. She drives a 1953 Plymouth sedan, a blue Tudor with a stove-in front fender on the right side. The license number is — '

Norman stopped listening. Why had he said there hadn't been anyone here? The man was describing that girl all right, he knew all about her. Well, he still couldn't prove the girl had come, if Norman denied it. And he'd have to keep on denying, now.

'No, I don't think I can help you.'

'Doesn't the description fit anyone who's been here during the past week? It's quite likely she would have registered under another name. Perhaps if you'd let me look over your register for a minute — '

Norman put his hand on the ledger and shook his head. 'Sorry, mister,' he said. 'I couldn't let you do that.'

'Maybe this will help change your mind.'

The man reached into his inside coat

pocket, and for a minute Norman wondered if he was going to offer him some money. The wallet came out, but the man didn't remove any bills. Instead he flipped it open and laid it on the counter, so Norman could read the card.

'Milton Arbogast,' the man said. 'Investigator for Parity Mutual.'

'You're a detective?'

He nodded. 'I'm here on business, Mr. — '

'Norman Bates.'

'Mr. Bates. My company wants me to locate this girl, and I'd appreciate your co-operation. Of course, if you refuse to let me inspect your register, I can always get in touch with the local authorities. I guess you know that.'

Norman didn't know, but he was sure of one thing. There mustn't be any local authorities to come snooping around. He hesitated, his hand still covering the ledger. 'What's this all about?' he asked. 'What did this girl do?'

'Stolen car,' Mr. Arbogast told him.

'Oh.' Norman was a little more relieved. For a moment he'd been afraid it was something serious, that the girl was missing or wanted for some major offense. In that case, there'd be a real investigation. But a missing car, particularly an old beat-up heap like that one —

'All right,' he said. 'Help yourself. I just wanted to make sure you had a legitimate reason.' He removed his hand.

'It's legitimate, all right.' But Mr. Arbogast didn't reach for the register right away. First he took an envelope out of his pocket and laid it down on the counter. Then he grabbed the ledger, turned it around, and thumbed down the list of signatures.

Norman watched his blunt thumb move, saw it stop suddenly and decisively.

'I thought you said something about not having any customers last Saturday or Sunday?'

'Well, I don't recall anyone. I mean, we might have had one or two, but there was no big business.'

'How about this one? This Jane Wilson, from San Antonio? She signed in on Saturday night.'

'Oh — come to think of it, you're right.' The pounding had started up in Norman's chest again, and he knew he'd made a mistake when he pretended not to recognize the description, but it was too late now. How could he possibly explain in such a way so that the detective wouldn't be suspicious? What was he going to say?

Right now the detective wasn't saying anything. He had picked up the envelope and

124

laid it alongside the ledger page, comparing the handwriting. That's why he'd brought the envelope out, it was in *her* handwriting! Now he'd know. He *did* know!

Norman could tell it when the detective raised his head and stared at him. Here, close up, he could see beneath the shadow cast by the hat brim. He could see the cold eyes, the eyes that *knew*.

'It's the girl, all right. This handwriting is identical.'

'It is? Are you sure?'

'Sure enough that I'm going to get a photostat made, even if it takes a court order. And that isn't all I can do, if you won't start talking and tell me the truth. Why did you lie about not seeing this girl?'

'I didn't lie. I just forgot — '

'You said you had a good memory.'

'Well, yes, generally I do. Only — '

'Prove it.' Mr. Arbogast lit a cigarette. 'In case you don't know, car theft is a federal offense. You wouldn't want to be involved as an accessory, would you?'

'Involved? How could I be involved? A girl drives in here, she takes a room, spends the night, and drives away again. How can I possibly be involved?'

'By withholding information.' Mr. Arbogast inhaled deeply. 'Come on, now, let's have it.

You saw the girl. What did she look like?'

'Just as you described her, I guess. It was raining hard when she came in. I was busy. I didn't really take a second look. I let her sign in, gave her a key, and that was that.'

'Did she say anything? What did you talk about?'

'The weather, I suppose. I don't remember.'

'Did she seem ill at ease in any way? Was there anything about her that made you suspicious?'

'No. Nothing at all. She seemed like just another tourist to me.'

'Good enough.' Mr. Arbogast ground his cigarette butt into the ash tray. 'Didn't impress you one way or the other, eh? On one hand, there was nothing to cause you to suspect anything was wrong with her. And on the other, she didn't particularly arouse your sympathies, either. I mean, you felt no emotion toward this girl at all.'

'Certainly not.'

Mr. Arbogast leaned forward, casually. 'Then why did you try to shield her by pretending you never remembered that she had come here?'

'I didn't try! I just forgot, I tell you.' Norman knew he'd walked into a trap, but he wasn't going any further. 'What are you trying to insinuate — do you think *I* helped her steal the car?'

'Nobody's accusing you of anything, Mr. Bates. It's just that I need all the facts I can get. You say she came alone?'

'She came alone, she took a room, she left the next morning. She's probably a thousand miles away by now — '

'Probably.' Mr. Arbogast smiled. 'But let's take it just a little slower, shall we? Maybe you can remember something. She left alone, is that it? About what time would you say?'

'I don't know. I was asleep up at the house Sunday morning.'

'Then you don't actually know she was *alone* when she left?'

'I can't prove it, if that's what you mean.'

'How about during the evening? Did she have any visitors?'

'No.'

'You're positive?'

'Quite positive.'

'Did anyone else happen to see her here that night?'

'She was the only customer.'

'And you were on duty alone?'

'That's right.'

'She stayed in her room?'

'Yes.'

'All evening? Didn't even make a phone call?'

'Of course not.'

'So you're the only one who knew she was here at all?'

'I've already told you that.'

'What about the old lady — did *she* see her?'

'What old lady?'

'The one up at the house, in back of here.'

Norman could feel the pounding now; his heart was going to beat its way right through his chest. He started to say, 'There is no old lady,' but Mr. Arbogast was still talking.

'I noticed her staring out of the window when I drove in. Who is she?'

'That's my mother.' He had to admit it, there was no way out. No way out. He could explain. 'She's pretty feeble, she never comes down here any more.'

'Then she didn't see the girl?'

'No. She's sick. She stayed in her room when we ate supp — '

It slipped out, just like that. Because Mr. Arbogast had asked the questions too fast, he'd done it on purpose just to confuse him, and when he mentioned Mother, it caught Norman off guard. He'd thought only about protecting *her*, and now —

Mr. Arbogast wasn't casual any more. 'You

128

had supper with Mary Crane, up at your house?'

'Just coffee and sandwiches. I — I thought I told you. It wasn't anything. You see, she asked where she could eat, and I said Fairvale, but that's almost twenty miles away, and it was raining, so I took her up to the house with me. That's all there was to it.'

'What did you talk about?'

'We didn't talk about anything. I told you Mother's sick, and I didn't want to disturb her. She's been sick all week. I guess that's what's been upsetting me, making me forget things. Like this girl, and having supper. It just slipped my mind.'

'Is there anything else that might have slipped your mind? Like say you and this girl coming back here and having yourself a little party — '

'No! Nothing like that! How can you say such a thing, what right have you got to say such a thing? I — I won't even talk to you any more. I've told you all you wanted to know. Now, get out of here!'

'All right.' Mr. Arbogast pulled down the brim of his Stetson. 'I'll be on my way. But first I'd like to have a word with your mother. Maybe she might have noticed something you've forgotten.'

'I tell you she didn't even *see* the girl!'

129

Norman came around the counter. 'Besides, you can't talk to her. She's very ill.' He could hear his heart pounding and he had to shout above it. 'I forbid you to see her.'

'In that case, I'll come back with a search warrant.'

He was bluffing, Norman knew it now. 'That's ridiculous! Nobody'd issue one. Who'd believe I'd want to steal an old car?'

Mr. Arbogast lit another cigarette and threw the match into the ash tray. 'I'm afraid you don't understand,' he said, almost gently. 'It isn't really the car at all. You might as well have the whole story. This girl — Mary Crane — stole forty thousand dollars in cash from a real estate firm in Fort Worth.'

'Forty thousand — '

'That's right. Skipped town with the money. You can see it's a serious business. That's why everything I can find out is important. That's why I'm going to insist on talking to your mother. With or without your permission.'

'But I've already told you she doesn't know anything, and she's not well, she's not well at all.'

'I promise I won't say anything to upset her.' Mr. Arbogast paused. 'Of course, if you want me to come back with the sheriff and a warrant — '

'No.' Norman shook his head hastily. 'You mustn't do that.' He hesitated, but there was nothing to hesitate about, now. *Forty thousand dollars. No wonder he'd asked so many questions. Of course he could get a warrant, no use making a scene. And besides, there was that Alabama couple down the line. No way out, no way at all.*

'All right,' Norman said. 'You can talk to her. But let me go up to the house first and tell her you're coming. I don't want you busting in without any explanation and getting her all excited.' He moved toward the door. 'You wait here, in case anyone drives in.'

'Okay.' Arbogast nodded, and Norman hurried out.

It wasn't much of a climb up the hill, but he thought he'd never make it. His heart pounded the way it had the other night, and it was just like the other night now, nothing had changed. No matter what you did, you couldn't get away from it. Not by trying to behave like a good boy and not by trying to behave like an adult, either. Nothing helped, because he was what he was, and that wasn't enough. Not enough to save him, and not enough to save Mother. If there was going to be any help at all now, it would have to come from her.

Then he unlocked the front door and climbed the stairs and went into her room, and he intended to speak to her very calmly, but when he saw her just sitting there by the window he couldn't hold it back. He began to shake and the sobs came tearing up out of his chest, the terrible sobs, and he put his head down against her skirt and he told her.

'All right,' Mother said. She didn't seem surprised at all. 'We'll take care of this. Just leave everything to me.'

'Mother — if you just talked to him for a minute, told him you don't know anything — he'd go away, then.'

'But he'd come back. Forty thousand dollars, that's a lot of money. Why didn't you tell me about it?'

'I didn't know. I swear it, I didn't know!'

'I believe you. Only *he* won't. He won't believe you and he won't believe me. He probably thinks we're all in on it together. Or that we did something to the girl, because of the money. Don't you see how it is?'

'Mother — ' He closed his eyes, he couldn't look at her. 'What are you going to do?'

'I'm going to get dressed. We want to be all ready for your visitor, don't we? I'll just take some things into the bathroom. You can go back and tell this Mr. Arbogast to come up now.'

'No, I can't. I won't bring him up here, not if you're going to — '

And he couldn't, he couldn't move at all, now. He wanted to faint, but even that wouldn't stop what was going to happen.

In just a few minutes, Mr. Arbogast would get tired of waiting. He'd walk up to the house alone, he'd knock on the door, he'd open it and come in. And when he did —

'Mother, please, *listen* to me!'

But she didn't listen, she was in the bathroom, she was getting dressed, she was putting on make-up, she was getting ready. *Getting ready.*

And all at once she came gliding out, wearing the nice dress with the ruffles. Her face was freshly powdered and rouged, she was pretty as a picture, and she smiled as she started down the stairs.

Before she was halfway down, the knocking came.

It was happening, Mr. Arbogast was here; he wanted to call out and warn him, but something was stuck in his throat. He could only listen as Mother cried gaily, 'I'm coming! I'm coming! Just a moment, now!'

And it *was* just a moment.

Mother opened the door and Mr. Arbogast

133

walked in. He looked at her and then he opened his mouth to say something. As he did so he raised his head, and that was all Mother had been waiting for. Her arm went out and something bright and glittering flashed back and forth, back and forth —

It hurt Norman's eyes and he didn't want to look. He didn't have to look, either, because he already knew.

Mother had found his razor . . .

10

Norman smiled at the elderly man and said, 'Here's your key. That'll be ten dollars for the two of you, please.'

The elderly man's wife opened her purse. 'I've got the money here, Homer.' She placed a bill on the counter, nodding at Norman. Then she stopped nodding and her eyes narrowed. 'What's the matter, don't you feel good?'

'I'm — I'm just a little tired, I guess. Be all right. Going to close up now.'

'So early? I thought motels stayed open until all hours. Particularly on Saturday nights.'

'We don't get much business here. Besides, it's almost ten.'

Almost ten. Nearly four hours. Oh, my God.

'I see. Well, good night to you.'

'Good night.'

They were going out now, and he could step away from the counter, he could switch off the sign and close the office. But first he was going to take a drink, a big drink, because he needed one. And it didn't matter whether he drank or not, nothing mattered now; it was all over. All over, or just beginning.

Norman had already taken several drinks. He took one as soon as he returned to the motel, around six, and he'd taken one every hour since then. If he hadn't, he would never have been able to last; never been able to stand here, knowing what was lying up there at the house, underneath the hall rug. That's where he'd left it, without trying to move anything; he just pulled up the sides of the rug and tossed them over to cover it. There was quite a bit of blood, but it wouldn't soak through. Besides, there was nothing else he *could* do, then. Not in broad daylight.

Now, of course, he'd have to go back. He'd given Mother strict orders not to touch anything, and he knew she'd obey. Funny, once it had happened, how she collapsed again. It seemed as if she'd nerve herself up to almost anything — the manic phase, wasn't that what they called it? — but once it was over, she just wilted, and he had to take over. He told her to go back to her room, and *not* to show herself at the window, just lie down until he got there. And he had locked the door.

But he'd have to unlock it now.

Norman closed the office and went

outside. There was the Buick, Mr. Arbogast's Buick, still parked just where he had left it.

Wouldn't it be wonderful if he could just climb into that car and drive away? Drive away from here, far away, and never come back again at all? Drive away from the motel, away from Mother, away from that thing lying under the rug in the hall?

For a moment the temptation welled up, but only for a moment; then it subsided and Norman shrugged. It wouldn't work, he knew that much. He could never get far enough away to be safe. Besides, that thing was waiting for him. Waiting for him —

So he glanced up and down the highway and then he looked at Number One and at Number Three to see if their blinds were drawn, and then he stepped into Mr. Arbogast's car and took out the keys he'd found in Mr. Arbogast's pocket. And he drove up to the house, very slowly.

All the lights were out. Mother was asleep in her room, or maybe she was only pretending to be asleep — Norman didn't care. Just so she stayed out of his way while he took care of this. He didn't want Mother around to make him feel like a little boy. He had a man's job to do. A grown man's job.

It took a grown man just to bundle the rug together and lift what was in it. He got it down the steps and into the back seat of the car. And he'd been right about there not being any leaking. These old shag rugs were absorbent.

When he got through the field and down to the swamp, he drove along the edge a way until he came to an open space. Wouldn't do to try and sink the car in the same place he'd put the other one. But this new spot was satisfactory, and he used the same method. It was really very easy, in a way. *Practice makes perfect*.

Except that there was nothing to joke about; not while he sat there on the tree stump and waited for the car to go down. It was worse than the other time — you'd think because the Buick was a heavier car that it would sink faster. But it took a million years. Until at last, *plop!*

There. It was gone forever. Like that girl, and the forty thousand dollars. Where had it been? Not in her purse, certainly, and not in the suitcase. Maybe in the overnight bag, or somewhere in the car. He should have looked, that's what he should have done. Except that he'd been in no condition to search, even if he'd known the money was there. And if he *had* found it, no telling what might have happened. Most probably he would have given himself away when the detective came around. You always gave yourself away if you had a guilty conscience. That was one thing to be thankful for — he wasn't responsible for all this. Oh, he knew all about being an accessory; on the other hand, he had to protect Mother. It meant protecting himself as well, but it was really Mother he was thinking about.

Norman walked back through the field, slowly. Tomorrow he'd have to return with the car and the trailer — do it all over again. But that wasn't half as important as attending to another matter.

Again, it was just a matter of watching out for Mother.

He'd thought it all through, and the facts just had to be faced.

Somebody was going to come here and inquire about that detective.

It just stood to reason, that's all. The company — something-or-other Mutual — that employed him wasn't going to let him disappear without an investigation. They probably had been in touch with him, or heard from him, all week long. And certainly the real-estate firm would be interested. Everybody was interested in forty thousand dollars.

So, sooner or later, there'd be questions to answer. It might be several days, or even a week, the way it had been with that girl. But he knew what was coming. And this time he was going to be prepared.

He had it all figured out. No matter who showed up, the story would be perfectly straight. He'd memorize it, rehearse it, so there'd be no slips of the tongue the way he had slipped tonight. Nobody was going to get him excited or confused; not if he knew in advance what to expect. Already he was planning just what to say when the time came.

The girl had stayed at the motel, yes. He'd admit that right away, but of course he hadn't suspected anything while she was here — not until Mr. Arbogast came, a week later. The girl had spent the night and driven away. There'd be no story about any conversation, and certainly nothing about eating together at the house.

What he *would* say, though, is that he'd told everything to Mr. Arbogast, and the only part which seemed to interest him was when he mentioned that the girl had asked him how far it was from here to Chicago, and could she make it in a single day?

That's what interested Mr. Arbogast. And he'd thanked him very much and climbed back into his car and driven off. Period. No, he had no idea where he was headed for. Mr.

Arbogast hadn't said. He just drove off. What time had it been? A little after suppertime, Saturday.

There it was, just a simple little statement of fact. No special details, nothing elaborate to arouse anyone's suspicions. A fugitive girl had passed this way and gone on. A week later a detective followed her trail, asked for and received information, then departed. Sorry, mister, that's all I know about it.

Norman knew he could tell it that way, tell it calmly and easily this time, because he wouldn't have to worry about Mother.

She wasn't going to be looking out of the window. In fact, she wasn't going to be in the house at all. Even if they came with one of those search warrants, they weren't going to find Mother.

That would be the best protection of all. Protection for her, even more than for him. He'd made up his mind on it, and he was going to see that it worked out. There was no sense in even waiting until tomorrow.

Strange, now that it was actually over, he still felt fully confident. It wasn't like the other time, when he'd gone to pieces and needed to know Mother was there. Now he needed to know she was *not* there. And he had the necessary gumption, for once, to tell her just that.

So he marched upstairs, in the dark, and went straight to her room. He switched on the light. She was in bed, of course, but not asleep; she hadn't been sleeping at all, just playing possum.

'Norman, where on earth have you been? I was so worried — '

'You know where I've been, Mother. Don't pretend.'

'Is everything all right?'

'Certainly.' He took a deep breath. 'Mother, I'm going to ask you to give up sleeping in your room for the next week or so.'

'What's that?'

'I said, I have to ask you not to sleep here for the next week or so.'

'Are you out of your mind? This is my room.'

'I know. And I'm not asking you to give it up permanently. Only for a little while.'

'But why on earth — '

'Mother, please listen and try to understand. We had a visitor here today.'

'Must you talk about that?'

'I must, for a moment. Because sooner or later, somebody will be around to inquire after him. And I'll say he came and left.'

'Of course that's what you'll say, son. That'll be the end of it.'

'Perhaps. I hope so. But I can't take chances. Maybe they'll want to search the house.'

'Let them. He won't be here.'

'Neither will you.' He gulped a breath, then rushed on. 'I mean it, Mother. It's for your own protection. I can't afford to let anyone see you, like that detective did today. I don't want anyone to start asking you questions — you know why as well as I do. It's just impossible. So the safest thing for both of us is to make sure you're just not around.'

'What are you going to do — bury me in the swamp?'

'Mother — '

She started to laugh. It was more like a cackle, and he knew that once she really got started she wouldn't stop. The only way to stop her was to outshout her. A week ago, Norman would never have dared. But this wasn't a week ago, it was *now*, and things were different. It was *now*, and he had to face the truth. Mother was more than sick. She was psychotic, dangerously so. He had to control her, and he would.

'Shut up!' he said, and the cackling ceased. 'I'm sorry,' he said softly. 'But you must listen to me. I've got it all figured out. I'm going to take you down into the fruit cellar.'

'The fruit cellar? Why, I can't — '

'You can. And you will. You have to. I'll see to it that you're taken care of, there's a light and I can put in a cot for you and — '

'I *won't!*'

'I'm not asking you, Mother. I'm telling you. You're going to stay in the fruit cellar until I think it's safe for you to come upstairs again. And I'll hang that old Indian blanket on the wall, so that it covers up the door. Nobody will notice a thing, even if they bother to go down into the cellar. It's the only way we can both be sure that you're going to be safe.'

'Norman, I refuse to even discuss it any further with you. I'm not going to budge from this room!'

'Then I'll have to carry you.'

'Norman, you wouldn't *dare* — '

But he did. Finally, that's just what he did. He picked her up right off the bed and carried her, and she was light as a feather compared to Mr. Arbogast, and she smelled of perfume instead of stale cigarette smoke, the way he had. She was too astonished to put up a fight, just whimpered a little. Norman was startled at how easy it was, once he made up his mind to go through with it. Why, she was just a sick old lady, a frail, feeble thing! He didn't have to be afraid of her, not really. *She* was afraid of *him*, now.

Yes, she must be. Because not once, all through this, had she called him 'son.'

'I'll fix the cot for you,' he told her. 'And there's a pot, too — '

'Norman, *must* you talk that way?' For just an instant she flared up in the old way, then subsided. He bustled around, bringing blankets, arranging the curtains on the small window so that there'd be sufficient ventilation. She began whimpering again, not so much whimpering as muttering under her breath.

'It's like a prison cell, that's what it is; you're trying to make a prisoner out of me. You don't love me any more, Norman, you don't love me or else you wouldn't treat me this way.'

'If I didn't love you, do you know where you'd be today?' He didn't want to say it, but he had to. 'The State Hospital for the Criminal Insane. That's where you'd be.'

He snapped out the light, wondering if she'd heard him, wondering if his words had gotten through to her, even if she did.

Apparently she understood. Because just as he closed the door she answered. Her voice was deceptively soft in the darkness, but somehow the words cut into him; cut into him more deeply than the straight razor had cut into Mr. Arbogast's throat.

'Yes, Norman, I suppose you're right. That's where I'd probably be. But I wouldn't be there alone.'

Norman slammed the door, locked it, and turned away. He wasn't quite sure, but as he ran up the cellar steps he thought he could still hear her chuckling gently in the dark.

11

Sam and Lila sat in the back room of the store, waiting for Arbogast to arrive. But all they heard were the sounds of Saturday night.

'You can tell when it's Saturday night in a town like this,' Sam commented. 'The noises are different. Take the traffic, for one thing. There's more of it, and it moves faster. That's because Saturday is the evening when the teen-agers get the cars.

'And all that rattling and squealing you hear — that's parking. Farm families in their old jalopies, coming in to see the show. Hired hands, in a hurry to head for the taverns.

'Notice the footsteps? They're different, too. Hear that running? The kids are loose. Saturday's the night they stay up late. No homework.' He shrugged. 'Of course, I suppose it's a lot more noisy in Fort Worth on any night of the week.'

'I suppose so,' Lila said. Then, 'Sam, why doesn't he get here? It's almost nine.'

'You must be hungry.'

'It isn't that. But why doesn't he come?'

'Maybe he's tied up, maybe he found out something important.'

'He could at least call. He knows how worried we are.'

'Just be patient a little while longer — '

'I'm sick of waiting!' Lila stood up, pushing back her chair. She began to pace back and forth across the narrow room. 'I never should have waited in the first place. I should have gone straight to the police. Wait, wait, wait — that's all I've heard, all week long! First Mr. Lowery, then Arbogast, and now you. Because you're all thinking about the money, not about my sister. Nobody cares what happens to Mary, nobody but me!'

'That's not true. You know how I feel about her.'

'Then how can you stand it? Why don't you *do* something? What kind of a man are you, sitting here and handing out cracker-barrel philosophy at a time like this?'

She grasped her purse and pushed past him.

'Where are you going?' Sam asked.

'To see that sheriff of yours, right now.'

'It would be just as easy to call him. After all, we want to be here when Arbogast shows up.'

'*If* he shows up. Maybe he's left town for good, if he's found something. He wouldn't have to come back.' Lila's voice teetered along a thin, hysterical edge.

Sam took her arm. 'Sit down,' he said. 'I'll phone the sheriff.'

She made no attempt to follow him as he walked out into the store. He went over to the rear counter, stood next to the cash register, and picked up the receiver.

'One-six-two, please. Hello, sheriff's office? This is Sam Loomis, over at the hardware store. I'd like to speak to Sheriff Chambers . . .

'He's *what*? No, I hadn't heard anything about it. Where did you say — Fulton? When do you suppose he'll be back? I see. No, nothing wrong. I just wanted to talk to him. Look, if he gets in any time before midnight, would you ask him to call me here at the store? I'll be here all night. Yes. Thanks, I'd appreciate that.'

Sam hung up and walked back into the rear room.

'What did he say?'

'He wasn't there.' Sam reported the conversation, watching her face as he spoke. 'Seems somebody robbed the bank over at Fulton around suppertime this evening. Chambers and the whole State Highway Patrol gang are out setting up roadblocks. That's what all the excitement's about. I talked to old Peterson; he's the only one left in the sheriff's office. There's two cops

149

walking the beat here in town, but they wouldn't be any use to us.'

'So now what are you going to do?'

'Why, wait, of course. Chances are, we won't be able to talk to the sheriff until tomorrow morning.'

'But don't you even care what happens to — '

'Of course I care.' He cut in on her sharply, deliberately. 'Would it ease your mind any if I called the motel and found out what's holding Arbogast up?'

She nodded.

Again he went back into the store. This time she accompanied him and stood waiting while he asked the operator for information. She finally located the name — Norman Bates — and found the number. Sam waited while she put the call through.

'Funny,' he said, hanging up. 'Nobody answers.'

'Then I'm going out there.'

'No, you're not.' He put his hand on her shoulder. 'I'm going out. You wait right here, in case Arbogast comes in.'

'Sam, what do you think happened?'

'I'll tell you when I get back. Now you just relax. It shouldn't take me more than three quarters of an hour.'

And it didn't, because Sam drove fast. In

exactly forty-two minutes he unlocked the front door, came into the store again. Lila was waiting for him.

'Well?' she asked.

'Funny. The place was closed up. No lights in the office. No lights in the house behind the motel. I went up there and banged on the door for five minutes straight, and nothing happened. The garage next to the house was open and empty. Looks like this Bates went away for the evening.'

'What about Mr. Arbogast?'

'His car wasn't there. Just two parked down at the motel — I looked at the licenses. Alabama and Illinois.'

'But where could — '

'The way I figure it,' Sam said, 'is that Arbogast *did* find out something. Maybe something important. It could be that he and Bates both went off together. And that's why we haven't gotten any word.'

'Sam, I can't take much more of this. I've got to know!'

'You've got to eat, too.' He displayed a bulging paper bag. 'Stopped in at the drive-in on my way back, brought us some hamburgers and coffee. Let's take the stuff into the back room.'

By the time they finished eating it was after eleven.

'Look,' Sam said. 'Why don't you go back to the hotel and get some rest? If anyone calls or comes in, I'll phone you. No sense in us both sitting around like this.'

'But — '

'Come on. Worrying isn't going to help. Chances are, I've figured it right. Arbogast *has* located Mary and we'll get news by morning. Good news.'

But there was no good news on Sunday morning.

By nine o'clock, Lila was rattling the front door of the hardware store.

'Hear anything?' she asked. And when Sam shook his head, she frowned. 'Well, I found out something. Arbogast checked out over at the hotel yesterday morning — *before* he even started to look around.'

Sam didn't say anything. He picked up his hat and walked out of the store with her.

The streets of Fairvale were empty on Sunday morning. The courthouse was set back in a square on Main Street, surrounded by a lawn on all four sides. One side contained a statue of a Civil War veteran — the kind cast up by the thousands back in the eighties to occupy courthouse lawns all over the country. The other three sides displayed, respectively, a Spanish-American War trench mortar, a World War I cannon, and a granite shaft bearing the names of fourteen Fairvale citizens who had died in World War II. Benches lined the sidewalks all around the square, but they were vacant at this hour.

The courthouse itself was closed, but the sheriff's office was over in the annex — Fairvale citizens still spoke of it as the 'new' annex, though it had been added back in 1946. The side door was open. They entered, climbed the stairs, walked down the hall to the office.

Old Peterson was doing duty at the outer desk, all alone.

'Morning, Sam.'

'Good morning, Mr. Peterson. Sheriff around?'

'Nope. Hear about them bank robbers? Busted right through the roadblock down at Parnassus. FBI's after 'em now. Sent an alert — '

'Where is he?'

'Well, he got in pretty late last night — early this morning, I should say.'

'Did you give him my message?'

The old man hesitated. 'I — I guess I forgot. All this excitement around here.' He wiped his mouth. ' 'Course I intended to, today, when he comes in.'

'What time will that be?'

'Right after lunch, I guess. Sunday mornings he's over to the church.'

'What church?'

'First Baptist.'

'Thanks.'

'You wouldn't go pulling him out of — '

Sam turned away without answering. Lila's high heels clattered hollowly beside him in the hall.

'What kind of a hick town is this, anyway?' she murmured. 'A bank is held up and the sheriff is in church. What's he doing, praying that somebody will catch the robbers for him?' Sam didn't answer. When they reached the street she turned to him again. 'Where are we going now?'

'First Baptist Church, of course.'

But it turned out that they didn't have to interrupt Sheriff Chambers at his devotions. As they turned down the side street it was apparent that the services had just ended; people were beginning to emerge from the steepled structure.

'There he is,' Sam muttered. 'Come on.'

He led her over to a couple who stood near the curbing. The woman was a short, gray-haired nonentity in a mail-order print dress; the man was tall, broad across the shoulders and paunchily protruding at the waistline. He wore a blue serge suit and his

154

red, seamed neck twisted in rebellion against the restraint of a white, starched collar. He had curly graying hair and curly black eyebrows.

'Hold on a minute, Sheriff,' said Sam. 'I'd like to talk to you.'

'Sam Loomis. How are you?' Sheriff Chambers held out a large red hand. 'Ma, you know Sam, here.'

'I'd like you to meet Lila Crane. Miss Crane is visiting here from Fort Worth.'

'Pleased to meet you. Say, you aren't the one old Sam keeps talking about, are you? Never let on you were so pretty — '

'It's my sister you're thinking of,' Lila told him. 'That's why we're here to see you.'

'I wonder if we could go over to your office for a minute,' Sam broke in. 'Then we can explain the situation.'

'Sure, why not?' Jud Chambers turned to his wife. 'Ma, why don't you take the car and go along home? I'll be over in a little while, soon's I'm finished with these folks.'

But it wasn't a little while. Once settled in Sheriff Chambers' office, Sam told his story. Even without interruptions, that took a good twenty minutes. And the Sheriff interrupted frequently.

'Now let me get this straight here,' he said, at the conclusion. 'This fella who came to you, this Arbogast. Why didn't he check with me?'

'I already explained that. He was hoping to avoid going to the authorities. His idea was to try and find Miss Crane and recover the money without any embarrassment to the Lowery Agency.'

'You say he showed you his credentials?'

'Yes.' Lila nodded. 'He was a licensed investigator for the insurance firm. And he managed to trace my sister all the way up here, to that motel. That's why we're so worried now, because he never came back, the way he said he would.'

'But he wasn't at the motel when you drove out there?' The question was addressed to Sam and he answered it.

'There was nobody there at all, Sheriff.'

'That's funny. Damned funny. I know this fella Bates who runs it. He's always there. Scarcely even leaves for an hour to come into town. You tried calling him this morning? Why don't you let me do that now? Probably turn out he was sound asleep when you got there last night.'

The big red hand picked up the phone.

'Don't tell him anything about the money,' Sam said. 'Just ask for Arbogast and see what he has to say.'

Sheriff Chambers nodded. 'Leave it to me,'

156

he murmured. 'I know how to handle this.'

He put through the call, and they waited.

'Hello . . . Bates? That you? This is Sheriff Chambers. That's right. I'm looking for a little information. Party here in town is trying to locate a fella name of Arbogast. Milton Arbogast, from Fort Worth. He's a special investigator or something for a firm called Parity Mutual.

'He what? Oh, he did? When was that? I see. What'd he have to say? It's all right, you can tell me, I already know all about it. Yeah . . .

'What's that again? Yeah. Yeah. And then he left, eh? Did he say where he was going? Oh, you think so? Sure. No, that's all . . .

'No, there's no trouble. Just that I thought he might check in here. Say, while I've got you, you don't think he might have stopped back later on in the evening, do you? What time you generally go to bed out there? Oh, I see. Well, I guess that just about covers it, then. Thanks for the information, Bates.'

He hung up and swiveled around to face them.

'Looks like your man headed for Chicago,' he said.

'Chicago?'

Sheriff Chambers nodded. 'Sure. That's where the girl said she was going. Your friend

157

Arbogast sounds like a pretty smooth operator to me.'

'What do you mean? What did this man Bates tell you just now?' Lila leaned forward.

'The same thing Arbogast told you yesterday evening when he called in from there. Your sister stayed at the motel last Saturday, but she didn't register under her own name. Called herself Jane Wilson, said she was from San Antonio. Let it slip that she was on her way to Chicago.'

'It couldn't have been Mary, then. Why she doesn't know anyone in Chicago; she's never been there in her life!'

'According to Bates, Arbogast was certain this was the girl. Even checked her handwriting. Her description, the car, everything fitted. Not only that, once he heard about Chicago, Bates says he took off from there like a bat out of hell.'

'But that's ridiculous! She has a week's start — *if* she was going there at all, that is. And he'd never find her in Chicago.'

'Maybe he knew where to look. Maybe he didn't tell you two *all* he'd found out about your sister and her plans.'

'What else could he know that we don't?'

'Never can tell about these smart operators. Could be he had some idea of just what your sister was up to. If he could get to her

158

and lay his hands on that money, he might not be so interested in reporting back to his company again.'

'Are you trying to say that Mr. Arbogast was a crook?'

'All I'm saying is that forty thousand in cash is a lot of money. And if Arbogast didn't show up here again, it means he had something figured out.' The Sheriff nodded. 'Must have been working the angles all along, the way it looks to me. Else why wouldn't he at least stop in here beforehand and see if I could help? You say he already checked out of the hotel yesterday.'

'Now wait a minute, Sheriff,' Sam said. 'You're jumping to conclusions. You've got nothing to go by except what this man Bates said over the phone just now. Couldn't he be lying?'

'Why should he? He told a straight story. Said the girl had been there, said Arbogast was there.'

'Where was he last night when I came, then?'

'Fast asleep in bed, just like I thought,' the Sheriff answered. 'Look here, I know this fella Bates. He's kind of an odd one in his way, not too bright, or at least that's how he always struck me. But he certainly isn't the type who'd ever pull any fast ones. Why shouldn't

159

I believe him? Particularly when I *know* your friend Arbogast was lying.'

'Lying? About what?'

'You told me what he said when he called you from the motel, last night. Well, that was just a stall. He must have already found out about Chicago, and he wanted to keep you quiet long enough for him to get a good head start. That's why he lied.'

'I don't understand, Sheriff. Just what did he lie about?'

'Why, when he said he was going up to see Norman Bates's mother. Norman Bates has no mother.'

'He hasn't?'

'Not for the last twenty years he hasn't. She's dead.' Sheriff Chambers nodded. 'Quite a scandal around these parts — surprised you don't remember it, but you were only a kid, then. She built this motel with a fella name of Considine, Joe Considine. She was a widow, understand, and the talk was that she and Considine were — ' The Sheriff stared at Lila, then broke off with an aimless wave of the hand. 'Anyways, they never did get married. Something must of went wrong, maybe she was in a family way, maybe Considine had a wife back where he came from. But one night they both took strychnine together. Regular poison pact, you might say. Her son, this

Norman Bates, he found them both. Guess it was pretty much of a shock. Way I remember it, he was laid up in the hospital for a couple of months, after. Didn't even go to the funeral. But I went. That's how I'm sure his mother is dead. Hell, I was one of the pallbearers!'

12

Sam and Lila had dinner over at the hotel.

It was not an enjoyable meal for either of them.

'I still can't believe Mr. Arbogast would go off without a word to us,' Lila said, putting down her coffee cup. 'And I can't believe Mary would go to Chicago, either.'

'Well, Sheriff Chambers believes it.' Sam sighed. 'And you've got to admit Arbogast lied to me about seeing Bates's mother.'

'Yes, I know. It doesn't make sense. On the other hand, neither does this story about Chicago. Mr. Arbogast didn't know any more about Mary than what we could tell him.'

Sam set his dessert spoon down next to the sherbet cup. 'I'm beginning to wonder how much any of us really knows about Mary,' he said. 'I'm engaged to her. You lived with her. Neither of us could believe she'd take that money. And yet there's no other answer. She did take it.'

'Yes.' Lila's voice was low. 'I believe that, now. She took the money. But she wouldn't do it for herself. Maybe she thought she could help you, maybe she wanted to bring it

162

to help pay off your debts.'

'Then why didn't she come to me? I wouldn't have accepted anything from her, even if I didn't know the money was stolen. But if she believed I might, then why didn't she come?'

'She did. At least, she got as far as that motel.' Lila crumpled her napkin, held it wadded tightly in her hand. 'That's what I was trying to tell the sheriff. We *know* she got as far as the motel. And just because Arbogast lied, that's no reason why this man Bates can't be lying, too. Why doesn't the sheriff at least go out there and take a look around for himself, instead of just talking to him on the phone?'

'I don't blame Sheriff Chambers for refusing,' Sam told her. 'How could he go any further? On what grounds, what evidence? What is he supposed to be looking for? You can't just go breaking in on people for no reason. Besides, they don't operate that way in a small town. Everybody knows everybody else, nobody wants to stir up trouble or cause unnecessary hard feeling. You heard what he said. There's nothing to make anyone suspect Bates. He's known him all his life.'

'Yes, and I've known Mary all my life. But there were some things about her *I* didn't suspect, either. He admitted this man was a little peculiar.'

'He didn't go that far. He said he was sort of a recluse. That's understandable, when you think of what a shock it must have been to him when his mother died.'

'His mother.' Lila frowned. 'That's the one thing I can't get through my head. If Arbogast wanted to lie, why should he lie about a thing like that?'

'I don't know. Maybe it was just the first thing he — '

'In fact, if he *was* planning to run off, then why did he bother to call up at all? Wouldn't it have been simpler to just leave, without our even knowing he'd actually been to that motel?' She let go of the napkin and stared at Sam. 'I — I'm beginning to get an idea.'

'What's up?'

'Sam, just what *did* Arbogast say there at the last, when he called you? About seeing Bates's mother?'

'He said that he'd noticed her sitting at the bedroom window when he drove in.'

'Maybe he wasn't lying.'

'But he had to be. Mrs. Bates is dead, you heard what the sheriff said.'

'Maybe it was Bates who lied. Perhaps Arbogast merely assumed that the woman was Bates's mother, and when he spoke of it, Bates said yes. He said she was sick, and nobody could see her, but Arbogast insisted.

Isn't that what he told you?'

'That's right. But I still don't see — '

'No, you don't. But Arbogast did. The point is, he saw *somebody* sitting in the window when he drove in. And maybe that somebody was — Mary.'

'Lila, you don't think that — '

'I don't know what to think. But why not? The trail ends there at the motel. Two people are missing. Isn't that enough? Isn't that enough for me, as Mary's sister, to go to the sheriff and insist that he make a thorough investigation?'

'Come on,' said Sam. 'Let's get going.'

They found Sheriff Chambers at his house, finishing dinner. He chewed on a toothpick while he listened to Lila's story.

'I dunno,' he said. 'You'd have to be the one to sign the complaint — '

'I'll sign anything you want. Just so you go out there and look around.'

'Couldn't we wait until tomorrow morning? I mean, I'm expecting word about those bank robbers and all, and — '

'Now, just a minute,' Sam said. 'This is a serious business, Sheriff. This girl's sister has been missing for over a week now. It isn't just a matter of money any more. For all we know, her life could be in danger. She could even be — '

'All right, all right! You don't have to tell me my business, Sam. Come on, let's go over to the office and I'll let her sign. But if you ask me, it's a waste of time. Norman Bates is no murderer.'

The word emerged, just like any other word, and died away. But its echo lingered. Sam heard it and Lila heard it. It stayed with them as they drove over to the courthouse annex with Sheriff Chambers. It stayed with them after the Sheriff drove away, out to the motel. He'd refused to take either of them along; told them to wait. So they waited in the office, just the two of them. The two of them — and the word.

It was late afternoon when he returned. He came in alone, giving them a look in which disgust and relief were equally compounded.

'Just what I told you,' he said. 'False alarm.'

'What did you — '

'Hold your horses, young lady. Give me a chance to sit down, I'll tell you all about it. Went straight out there and didn't run into any trouble at all. Bates, he was down in the woods behind the house, getting himself some kindling. I never even had to show the warrant — he was nice as pie. Told me to go look around for myself, even gave me the keys to the motel.'

'And did you look?'

'Of course I did. I went into every unit of the motel, and I covered that house of his from top to bottom. Didn't find a soul. Didn't find anything. Because there's nobody there. Nobody's been there, except Bates. He's lived alone all these years.'

'What about the bedroom?'

'There's a bedroom up front on the second floor, all right, and it used to be his mother's, when she was alive. That part's straight enough. In fact, he even kept it the way it was. Says he has no other use for it, seeing as how he's got the whole house to himself. Guess he's kind of an odd one, that Bates, but who wouldn't be, living alone like that all these years?'

'Did you ask him about what Arbogast told me?' Sam murmured. 'About seeing his mother when he drove in, and all that?'

'Sure, right away. He says it's a lie — Arbogast never even mentioned seeing anyone. I talked kind of rough to him at first, on purpose, just to see if there was something he was holding back on, but his story makes sense. I asked him about this Chicago business again, too. And I still think that's the real answer.'

'I can't believe it,' Lila said. 'Why would Mr. Arbogast make up that unnecessary excuse about seeing Bates's mother?'

'You'll have to ask him, next time you see him,' Sheriff Chambers told her. 'Maybe he saw her ghost sitting in the window.'

'You're *sure* his mother is dead?'

'I've already told you I was there, at the funeral. I saw the note she left for Bates when she and this Considine fella killed themselves. What more do you want? Do I have to dig her up and show her to you?' Chambers sighed. 'I'm sorry, miss. Didn't mean to fly off that way. But I've done all I can. I searched the house. Your sister isn't there, this man Arbogast isn't there. Didn't find a trace of their cars, either. Seems to me the answer's pretty plain. Anyway, I've done all I can.'

'What would you advise me to do, now?'

'Why, check with this fella Arbogast's home office, see if they know anything. Maybe they've got some lead on this Chicago angle. Don't suppose you can contact anyone until tomorrow morning, though.'

'I guess you're right.' Lila stood up. 'Well, thank you for all your trouble. I'm sorry to be such a bother.'

'That's what I'm here for. Right, Sam?'

'Right,' Sam answered.

Sheriff Chambers stood up. 'I know how you feel about all this, miss,' he said. 'I wish I could have been more of a help to you. But there's just nothing solid for me to go on. If you only had some kind of real evidence, now, then maybe — '

'We understand,' Sam said. 'And we both appreciate your co-operation.' He turned to Lila. 'Shall we go now?'

'You look into this Chicago business,' the big man called after them. 'So long, now.'

Then they were on the sidewalk. The late afternoon sun cast slanting shadows. As they stood there the black tip of the Civil War veteran's bayonet grazed Lila's throat.

'Want to come back to my place?' Sam suggested.

The girl shook her head.

'The hotel?'

'No.'

'Where would you like to go, then?'

'I don't know about you,' Lila said. 'But I'm going out to that motel.'

She raised her face defiantly, and the sharp shadow line slashed across her neck. For a moment, it looked as though somebody had just cut off Lila's head . . .

13

Norman knew they were coming, even before he saw them driving in.

He didn't know *who* they'd be, or what they'd look like, or even how many of them would come. But he knew they were coming.

He'd known it ever since last night when he lay in bed and listened to the stranger pound on the door. He had stayed very quiet, not even getting up to peek through the upstairs window. In fact, he'd even put his head under the covers while he waited for the stranger to go away. Finally, he *did* leave. It was lucky that Mother was locked in the fruit cellar. Lucky for him, lucky for her, lucky for the stranger.

But he'd known, then, that this wouldn't be the end of it. And it wasn't. This afternoon, when he was down at the swamp again, cleaning up, Sheriff Chambers had driven in.

It gave Norman quite a start, seeing the Sheriff again, after all these years. He remembered him very well, from the time of the nightmare. That's the way Norman always thought about Uncle Joe Considine and the poison and everything — it had been a long,

long nightmare from the moment he phoned the Sheriff until months afterward, when they let him out of the hospital to come back here to the house once more.

Seeing Sheriff Chambers now was like having the same nightmare all over, but people *do* have the same nightmare again and again. And the important thing to remember was that Norman had fooled the Sheriff the first time, when everything had been much harder. This time it should be even easier, if he just remembered to be calm. It should be, and it was.

He answered all the questions, he gave the Sheriff the keys, he let him search the house alone. That was even funny, in a way — letting the Sheriff go up to the house and search while Norman stayed down at the edge of the swamp and finished smoothing out all the footprints. It was funny, that is, as long as Mother kept quiet. If she thought Norman was down there in the cellar, if she cried out or made a sound, then there'd be real trouble. But she wouldn't do that, she had been warned, and besides the Sheriff wasn't even looking for Mother. He thought she was dead and buried.

How he'd fooled him the first time! Yes, and he fooled him just as easily again, because the Sheriff came back and he hadn't noticed a thing. He asked Norman some more questions about the girl and Arbogast and going to Chicago. Norman was tempted to invent a little more — maybe even say that the girl had mentioned staying at a certain hotel up there — but on second thought he realized it wouldn't be wise. It was better to just stick to what he'd already made up. The Sheriff believed that. He almost apologized before he went away.

So that part was settled, but Norman knew there'd be more. Sheriff Chambers hadn't come out here just on his own initiative. He wasn't following up any hunch — he couldn't be, because he hadn't known anything. His phone call yesterday was the tipoff. It meant somebody else knew about Arbogast and the girl. They got Sheriff Chambers to call. They sent the stranger out here last night, to snoop. They sent the Sheriff out today. And the next step would be to come out themselves. It was inevitable. Inevitable.

When Norman thought about that, his heart started up again. He wanted to do all sorts of crazy things — run away, go down into the cellar and put his head in Mother's lap, go upstairs and pull the covers back over his head. But none of this would help. He couldn't run away and leave Mother, and he couldn't risk taking her with him, now; not in her condition. He couldn't even go to her for comfort or advice. Up until last week, that's just what he would have done, but he didn't trust her any more, couldn't trust her after what had happened. And pulling the covers over his head wouldn't help.

If they came here again, he'd have to face them. That was the only sensible solution. Just face them, stick to his story, and nothing would happen.

But meanwhile he had to do something about the way his heart pounded.

He sat there in the office, all alone. Alabama had pulled out early this morning, and Illinois had left right after lunch. There were no new customers. It was beginning to cloud up again, and if the storm came he needn't expect any business this evening. So one drink wouldn't hurt. Not if it made his heart calm down again.

Norman found a bottle in the cubbyhole under the counter. It was the second bottle of the three he'd put there over a month ago. That wasn't bad; just the second bottle. Drinking the first one had gotten him into all this trouble, but it wouldn't happen that way again. Not now, when he could be sure Mother was safely out of the way. In a little while, when it got dark, he'd see about fixing her some dinner. Maybe tonight they could talk. But right now, he needed this drink. These drinks. The first didn't really help, but the second did the trick. He was quite relaxed now. Quite relaxed. He could even take a third one if he wanted to.

And then he wanted to very much, because he saw the car drive in.

It had nothing to distinguish it from any other car, no out-of-state license or anything like that, but Norman knew right away that *they* were here. When you're a psychic sensitive, you can *feel* the vibrations. And you can feel your heart pound, so you gulp the drink and watch them get out of the car. The man was ordinary-looking, and for a moment Norman wondered if he hadn't made a mistake. But then he saw the girl.

He saw the girl, and he tilted the bottle up — tilted it up to take a hasty swallow and to hide her face at the same time — because it was *the* girl.

She'd come back, out of the swamp!

No. No, she couldn't. That wasn't the answer, it couldn't be. Look at her again. Now, in the light. Her hair wasn't the same color at all, really; it was brownish blonde. And she wasn't as heavy. But she looked enough like the girl to be her sister.

Yes, of course. That must be who she was. And it explained everything. This Jane Wilson or whatever her real name was had run away with that money. The detective came after her, and now her sister. That was the answer.

He knew what Mother would do in a case like this. But thank God he'd never have to run *that* risk again. All he had to do was stick to his story and they'd go away. Just remember nobody could find anything, nobody could prove anything. And there was nothing to worry about, now that he knew what to expect.

The liquor had helped. It helped him to stand patiently behind the counter while he waited for them to come in. He could see them talking together outside the office, and that didn't bother him. He could see the dark clouds coming on out of the west, and that didn't bother him either. He saw the sky darken as the sun surrendered its splendor. *The sun surrendered its splendor* — why, it was like poetry; he was a poet! Norman smiled. He was many things. If they only knew —

But they didn't know, and they wouldn't know, and right now he was just a fat, middle-aged motel proprietor who blinked up at the pair of them as they came in and said, 'Can I help you?'

The man came up to the counter. Norman braced himself for the first question, then blinked again when the man didn't ask it. Instead he was saying, 'Could we have a room, please?'

Norman nodded, unable to answer. Had he made a mistake? But no, now the girl was stepping forward, and she *was* the sister, no doubt about it.

'Yes. Would you like to — '

'No, that's not necessary. We're anxious to get into some clean clothes.'

It was a lie. Their clothing was fresh. But Norman smiled. 'All right. It's ten dollars, double. If you'll just sign here and pay me now — '

He pushed the register forward. The man hesitated for a moment, then scribbled. Norman had had long practice when it came to reading names upside down. *Mr. and Mrs. Sam Wright. Independence, Mo.*

That was another lie. Wright was wrong. Filthy, stupid liars! They thought they were so clever, coming in here and trying to pull their tricks on him. Well, they'd see!

The girl was staring at the register now. Not at the name the man had written, but at another one, up on top of the page. Her sister's name. *Jane Wilson*, or whatever it was.

She didn't think he noticed when she squeezed the man's arm, but he did.

'I'll give you Number One,' Norman said.

176

'Where is that?' the girl asked.

'Down at the end.'

'How about Number Six?'

Number Six. Norman remembered now. He'd written it down, as he always did after each signature. Number Six had been the room he'd given the sister, of course. She'd noticed that.

'Number Six is up at this end,' he said. 'But you wouldn't want that. The fan's broken.'

'Oh, we won't need a fan. Storm's coming up, it'll cool off in a hurry.' *Liar.* 'Besides, six is our lucky number. We were married on the sixth of this month.' *Dirty, filthy liar.*

Norman shrugged. 'All right,' he said.

And it *was* all right. Now that he thought it over, it was even *better* than all right. Because if that's the way the liars were going to play it, if they weren't going to come out with any questions but just sneak around, then Number Six was ideal. He didn't have to worry about them finding anything in there. And he could keep an eye on them. Yes, he could keep an eye on them. Perfect!

So he took the key and he escorted them next door to Number Six. It was only a few steps, but already the wind had come up and it felt chilly there in the twilight. He unlocked the unit while the man brought out a bag. One ridiculous little bag, all the way from

Independence. *Nasty, rotten liars!*

He opened the door and they stepped in. 'Will there be anything else?' he asked.

'No, we're all right now, thank you.'

Norman closed the door. He went back to the office and took another drink. A congratulatory drink. This was going to be even easier than he'd dreamed. It was going to be easy as pie.

Then he tilted the license in its frame and stared through the crack into the bathroom of Number Six.

They weren't occupying it, of course; they were in the bedroom beyond. But he could hear them moving around, and once in a while he caught muffled phrases of their conversation. The two of them were searching for something. What it was he couldn't imagine. Judging from what he overheard, they weren't even sure, themselves.

' . . . help if we knew what we were looking for.' *The man's voice.*

And then, the girl's. ' . . . anything happened, there'd be something he overlooked. I'm sure of it. Crime laboratories you read about . . . always little clues . . . '

Man's voice again. 'But we're not detectives. I still think . . . better to talk to him . . . come right out, frighten him into admitting . . . '

Norman smiled. They weren't going to frighten *him* into anything. Any more than they were going to find anything. He'd been over that room thoroughly, from top to bottom. There were no telltale signs of what had happened, not the tiniest stain of blood, not a single hair.

Her voice, coming closer now. ' . . . understand? If we only *could* find something to go on, then we'd be able to scare him so that he'd talk.'

She was walking into the bathroom now, and he was following her. 'With any kind of evidence at all we could make the Sheriff come out. The State Police do that kind of laboratory work, don't they?'

He was standing in the doorway of the bathroom, watching her as she examined the sink. 'Look how clean everything is! I tell you, we'd better talk to him. It's our only chance.'

She had stepped out of Norman's field of vision. She was looking into the shower stall now, he could hear the curtains swishing back. The little bitch, she was just like her sister, she had to go into the shower. Well, let her, Let her and be damned!

' . . . not a sign . . . '

Norman wanted to laugh out loud. Of course there wasn't a sign! He waited for her to step out of the shower stall, but she didn't reappear. Instead he heard a sudden thumping noise.

'What are you doing?'

It was the man who asked the question, but Norman echoed it. What *was* she doing?

'Just reaching around in back here, behind the stall. You never know . . . Sam. Look! I've found something!'

She was standing in front of the mirror again, holding something in her hand. What was it, what had the little bitch found?

'Sam, it's an earring. One of Mary's earrings!'

'Are you sure?'

No, it couldn't be the other earring. It couldn't be.

'Of course it's one of hers. I ought to know. I gave them to her myself, for her birthday, last year. There's a custom jeweler who runs a little hole-in-the-wall shop in Dallas. He specializes in making up individual pieces — just one of a kind, you know. I had him do these for her. She thought it was terribly extravagant of me, but she loved them.'

He was holding the earring under the light now, staring at it as she spoke.

'She must have knocked it off when she was taking her shower and it fell over in back of the stall. Unless something else happ

— Sam, what's the matter?'

'I'm afraid something did happen, Lila. Do you see this? Looks to me like dried blood.'

'Oh — *no!*'

'Yes. Lila, you were right.'

The bitch. They were all bitches. Listen to her, now.

'Sam, we've got to get into that house. We've *got* to.'

'That's a job for the Sheriff.'

'He wouldn't believe us, even if we showed him this. He'd say she fell, bumped her head in the shower, something like that.'

'Maybe she did.'

'Do you really believe that, Sam? Do you?'

'No.' He sighed. 'I don't. But it still isn't proof that Bates had anything to do with — whatever did happen here. It's up to the Sheriff to find out more.'

'But he won't do anything, I know he won't! We'd have to have something that would really convince him, something from the house. I know we could find something there.'

'No. Too dangerous.'

'Then let's find Bates, show this to him. Maybe we can make him talk.'

'Yes, and maybe we can't. If he *is* involved, do you think he's just going to break down and confess? The smartest thing to do is go after the Sheriff, right now.'

'What if Bates is suspicious? If he sees us leave, he might run away.'

'He doesn't suspect us, Lila. But if you're worried, we could just put through a call — '

'The phone is in the office. He'd hear us.' Lila paused for a moment. 'Listen, Sam. Let *me* go after the Sheriff. You stay here and talk to Bates.'

'And accuse him?'

'Certainly not! Just go in and talk to him while I leave. Tell him I'm running into town to go to the drugstore, tell him anything, just so he doesn't get alarmed and stays put. Then we can be sure of things.'

'Well — '

'Give me the earring, Sam.'

The voices faded, because they were going back into the other room. The voices faded, but the words remained. The man was staying here while *she* went and got the Sheriff. That's the way it was going to be. And he couldn't stop her. If Mother was here, she'd stop her. She'd stop them both. But Mother wasn't here. She was locked up in the fruit cellar.

Yes, and if that little bitch showed the Sheriff the bloody earring, he'd come back and look for Mother. Even if he didn't find her in the cellar, he might get an idea. For twenty years now he hadn't even dreamed the truth, but he might, now. He might do the one thing Norman had always been afraid he'd do. He might find out what really happened the night Uncle Joe Considine died.

There were more sounds coming from next door. Norman adjusted the license frame hastily; he reached for the bottle again. But there was no time to take another drink, not now. Because he could hear the door slam, they were coming out of Number Six, she was going to the car and he was walking in here.

He turned to face the man, wondering what he was going to say.

But even more, he was wondering what the Sheriff would do. *The Sheriff could go up to Fairvale Cemetery and open Mother's grave. And when he opened it, when he saw the empty coffin, then he'd know the real secret.*

He'd know that Mother was alive.

There was a pounding in Norman's chest, a pounding that was drowned out by the first rumble of thunder as the man opened the door and came in.

14

For a moment Sam hoped that the sudden thunder would muffle the sound of the car starting in the driveway. Then, he noticed that Bates was standing at the end of the counter. From that position he could see the entire driveway and a quarter of a mile up the road. So there was no sense trying to ignore Lila's departure.

'Mind if I come in for a few minutes?' Sam asked. 'Wife's taking a little ride into town. She's fresh out of cigarettes.'

'Used to have a machine here,' Bates answered. 'But there wasn't enough call for them, so they yanked it out.' He peered over Sam's shoulder, gazing off into the dusk, and Sam knew he was watching the car move onto the highway. 'Too bad she has to go all that way. Looks as if it's going to be raining pretty hard in a few minutes.'

'Get much rain around here?' Sam sat down on the arm of a battered sofa.

'Quite a bit.' Bates nodded vaguely. 'We get all kinds of things around here.'

What did he mean by that remark? Sam peered up at him in the dim light. The eyes behind the fat man's glasses seemed vacant. Suddenly Sam caught the telltale whiff of alcohol, and at the same moment he noticed the bottle standing at the edge of the counter. That was the answer; Bates was a little bit drunk. Just enough to immobilize his expression, but not enough to affect his awareness. He caught Sam looking at the whiskey bottle.

'Care for a drink?' he was asking. 'Just about to pour a little one for myself when you came in.'

Sam hesitated. 'Well — '

'Find you a glass. There's one under here someplace.' He bent behind the counter, emerged holding a shot-glass. 'Don't generally bother with them, myself. Don't generally take a drink when I'm on duty, either. But with the damp coming on, a little something helps, particularly if you have rheumatism the way I do.'

He filled the shot-glass, pushed it forward on the counter. Sam rose and walked over to it.

'Besides, there won't be any more customers coming along in this rain. Look at it come down!'

Sam turned. It was raining hard, now; he couldn't see more than a few feet up the road in the downpour. It was getting quite dark, too, but Bates made no movement to switch on any lights.

'Go ahead, take your drink and sit down,' Bates said. 'Don't worry about me. I like to stand here.'

Sam returned to the sofa. He glanced at his watch. Lila had been gone about eight minutes now. Even in this rain, she'd get to Fairvale in less than twenty — then ten minutes to find the Sheriff, or say fifteen just to be on the safe side — twenty minutes more to return. Still, it would be better than three quarters of an hour. That was a long time to stall. What could he talk about?

Sam lifted his glass. Bates was taking a swig out of the bottle. He made a gulping noise.

'Must get pretty lonesome out here sometimes,' Sam said.

'That's right.' The bottle thumped down on the counter. 'Pretty lonesome.'

'But interesting, too, in a way, I suppose. I'll bet you get to see all kinds of people in a spot like this.'

'They come and go. I don't pay much attention. After a while you hardly notice.'

'Been here a long time?'

'Over twenty years, running the motel. I've always lived here, all my life.'

'And you run the whole place by yourself?'

'That's right.' Bates moved around the

counter, carrying the bottle. 'Here, let me fill up your glass.'

'I really shouldn't.'

'Won't hurt you. I'm not going to tell your wife.' Bates chuckled. 'Besides, I don't like to drink alone.'

He poured, then retreated behind the counter.

Sam sat back. The man's face was only a gray blur in the growing darkness. The thunder sounded overhead again, but there was no lightning. And here inside everything seemed quiet and peaceful.

Looking at this man, listening to him, Sam was beginning to feel slightly ashamed. He sounded so — so damned *ordinary!* It was hard to imagine him being mixed up in something like this.

And just what was he mixed up in, anyway, if he *was* mixed up? Sam didn't know. Mary had stolen some money, Mary had been here overnight, she had lost an earring in the shower. But she could have banged her head, she could have cut her ear when the earring came off. Yes, and she could have gone on to Chicago, too, just the way Arbogast and the Sheriff seemed to think. He really didn't know very much about Mary, when he came right down to it. In a way, her sister seemed more familiar. A nice girl, but too hair-triggered, too impulsive. Always making snap judgments and decisions. Like this business of wanting to run straight up and search Bates's house. Good thing he'd talked her out of that one. Let her bring the Sheriff. Maybe even that was a mistake. The way Bates was acting now, he didn't seem like a man who had anything on his conscience.

Sam remembered that he was supposed to be talking. It wouldn't do to just sit here.

'You were right,' he murmured. 'It is raining pretty hard.'

'I like the sound of the rain,' Bates said. 'I like the way it comes down hard. It's exciting.'

'Never thought of it in that way. Guess you can use a little excitement around here.'

'I don't know. We get our share.'

'We? I thought you said you lived here alone.'

'I said I operated the motel alone. But it belongs to both of us. My mother and me.'

Sam almost choked on the whiskey. He lowered the glass, clenching it tightly in his fist. 'I didn't know — '

'Of course not, how could you? Nobody does. That's because she always stays in the house. She has to stay there. You see, most people think she's dead.'

The voice was calm. Sam couldn't see Bates's face in the dimness now, but he knew it was calm, too.

'Actually, there *is* excitement around here, after all. Like there was twenty years ago, when Mother and Uncle Joe Considine drank the poison. I called the Sheriff and he came out and found them. Mother left a note, explaining everything. Then they had an inquest, but I didn't go to it. I was sick. Very sick. They took me to the hospital. I was in the hospital a long time. Almost too long to do any good when I got out. But I managed.'

'Managed?'

Bates didn't reply, but Sam heard the gurgle and then the bottle's thump.

'Here,' Bates said. 'Let me pour you another.'

'Not yet.'

'I insist.' He was coming around the counter now, and his shadowy bulk loomed over Sam. He reached for Sam's glass.

Sam drew back. 'First tell me the rest,' he said quickly.

Bates halted. 'Oh, yes. I brought Mother back home with me. That was the exciting part, you see — going out to the cemetery at night and digging up the grave. She'd been shut up in that coffin for such a long time that at first I thought she really *was* dead. But

189

she wasn't, of course. She couldn't be. Or else she wouldn't have been able to communicate with me when I was in the hospital all that while. It was only a trance state, really; what we call suspended animation. I knew how to revive her. There *are* ways, you know, even if some folks call it magic. Magic — that's just a label, you know. Completely meaningless. It wasn't so very long ago that people were saying that electricity was magic. Actually, it's a force, a force which can be harnessed if you know the secret. Life is a force, too, a vital force. And like electricity, you can turn it off and on, off and on. I'd turned it off, and I knew how to turn it on again. Do you understand me?'

'Yes — it's very interesting.'

'I thought you might be interested. You and the young lady. She isn't really your wife, is she?'

'Why — '

'You see, I know more than you think I know. And more than *you* know, yourself.'

'Mr. Bates, are you quite sure you're all right? I mean — '

'I know what you mean. You think I'm drunk, don't you? But I wasn't drunk when you came here. I wasn't drunk when you found that earring and told the young lady to go to the Sheriff.'

'I — '

'Sit still, now. Don't be alarmed. I'm not alarmed, am I? And I would be, if anything was wrong. But nothing is wrong. You don't think I'd tell you all this if there was anything wrong, do you?' The fat man paused. 'No, I waited until you came in. I waited until I saw her drive up the road. I waited until I saw her stop.'

'Stop?' Sam tried to find the face in the darkness, but all he could hear was the voice.

'Yes. You didn't know that she stopped the car, did you? You thought she went on to get the Sheriff, the way you told her. But she has a mind of her own. Remember what she wanted to do? She wanted to take a look at the house. And that's what she did do. That's where she is, now.'

'Let me out of here — '

'Of course. I'm not hindering you. It's just that I thought you might like another drink, while I told you the rest about Mother. The reason I thought you might like to know is because of the girl. She'll be meeting Mother, now.'

'Get out of my way!'

Sam rose, swiftly, and the blurred bulk fell back.

'You don't want another drink, then?' Bates's voice sounded petulantly over his

191

shoulder. 'Very well. Have it your own w — '

The end of his sentence was lost in the thunder, and the thunder was lost in the darkness as Sam felt the bottle explode against the roof of his skull. Then voice, thunder, explosion, and Sam himself all disappeared into the night . . .

★ ★ ★

And it was still night, but somebody was shaking him and shaking him; shaking him up out of the night and into this room where the light burned, hurting his eyes and making him blink. But Sam could feel now, and somebody's arms were around him, lifting him up, so that at first he felt as if his head would drop off. Then it was only throbbing, throbbing, and he could open his eyes and look at Sheriff Chambers.

Sam was sitting on the floor next to the sofa and Chambers was gazing down at him. Sam opened his mouth.

'Thank God,' he said. 'He was lying about Lila, then. She did get to you.'

The Sheriff didn't seem to be listening. 'Got a call from the hotel about half an hour ago. They were trying to locate your friend Arbogast. Seems he checked out, but he never took his bags with him. Left 'em downstairs Saturday morning, said he'd be back, but he never showed. Got to thinking it over, and then I tried to find you. Had a hunch you might have come out here on your own — lucky I followed through.'

'Then Lila didn't notify you?' Sam tried to stand up. His head was splitting.

'Take it easy, there.' Sheriff Chambers pushed him back. 'No, I haven't seen her at all. Wait — '

But this time Sam managed to make it. He stood on his feet, swaying.

'What happened here?' the Sheriff muttered. 'Where's Bates?'

'He must have gone up to the house after he slugged me,' Sam told him. 'They're up there now, he and his mother.'

'But she's dead — '

'No, she isn't,' Sam murmured. 'She's alive, the two of them are up at the house with Lila!'

'Come on.' The big man ploughed out into the rain. Sam followed him, scrambling along the slippery walk, panting as they began the ascent of the steep slope leading to the house beyond.

'Are you sure?' Chambers called over his shoulder. 'Everything's dark up there.'

'I'm sure,' Sam wheezed. But he might have saved his breath.

The thunder came suddenly and sharply, and the other sound was fainter and much more shrill. Yet both of them heard it, somehow, and both of them recognized it.

Lila was screaming.

15

Lila went up the steps, reaching the porch just before the rain came.

The house was old, its frame siding gray and ugly here in the half-light of the coming storm. Porch boards creaked under her feet, and she could hear the wind rattling the casements of the upstairs windows.

She rapped on the front door angrily, not expecting any answer from within. She didn't expect anyone to do anything any more.

The truth was that nobody else really *cared*. They didn't care about Mary at all, not a one of them. Mr. Lowery just wanted his money back, and Arbogast was only doing a job trying to find it for him. As for the Sheriff, all he was interested in was avoiding trouble. But it was Sam's reaction that really upset her.

Lila knocked again, and the house groaned a hollow echo. The sound of the rain drowned it out, and she didn't bother to listen closely.

All right, she *was* angry, she admitted it — and why shouldn't she be? A whole week of listening to *take it easy, be calm, relax, just be patient*. If they had their way, she'd still be back there in Fort Worth, she wouldn't have even come up here. But at least she'd counted on Sam to help her.

She might have known better. Oh, he seemed nice enough, even attractive in a way, but he had that slow, cautious, conservative small-town outlook. He and the Sheriff made a good pair. *Don't take any chances*, that was their whole idea.

Well, it wasn't hers. Not after she'd found the earring. How could Sam shrug it off and tell her to go get the Sheriff again? Why didn't he just grab Bates and beat the truth out of him? That's what she would have done, if she were a man. One thing was certain, she was through depending on others — others who didn't care, who just wanted to keep out of trouble. She didn't trust Sam to stick his neck out any more, and she certainly didn't trust the Sheriff.

If she hadn't gotten so angry she wouldn't be doing this, but she was sick of their caution, sick of their theories. There are times when you must stop analyzing and depend on your emotions. It was sheer emotion — frustration, to be exact — which prompted her to keep on with the hopeless task of rummaging around until she found Mary's earring. And there'd be something else here in the house. There *had* to be. She wasn't going to be foolish about this, she'd keep her head, but she was going to see for herself. Then it would be time enough to let Sam and the Sheriff take over.

Just thinking about their smugness made her rattle the doorknob. That wouldn't do any good. There was nobody inside the house to answer her, she already knew that. And she wanted in. That was the problem.

Lila dipped into her purse. All those tired old gags about how a woman's purse contains everything — the kind of gags that hicks like Sam and the Sheriff would appreciate. Nail file? No, that wouldn't do. But somewhere or other, she remembered, she'd picked up a skeleton key. It might be in the coin compartment, which she never used. Yes, here it was.

Skeleton key. Why did they have to call it that? Never mind, she wasn't going to worry about problems in philology now. The only problem was whether this key would work.

She inserted it in the lock and turned it part way. The lock resisted, and she reversed the motion. The key almost fitted, but there was something —

Again, anger came to her aid. She twisted the key sharply. It snapped at the handle with a brittle click, but the lock gave. She turned the doorknob, felt the door move away from her hand. It was open.

Lila stood in the hall. It was darker inside the house than out there on the porch. But there must be a light switch somewhere along the wall here.

She found it, snapped it on. The unshaded overhead bulb gave off a feeble, sickly glare against the background of peeling, shredded wallpaper. What was the design — bunches of grapes, or were they violets? Hideous. Like something out of the last century.

A glance into the parlor confirmed the observation. Lila didn't bother to go in. The rooms on this floor could wait until later. Arbogast had said he saw someone looking out of a window upstairs. That would be the place to begin.

There was no light switch for the stairway. Lila went up slowly, groping along the banister. As she reached the landing, the thunder came. The whole house seemed to shake with it. Lila gave an involuntary shudder, then relaxed. It *was* involuntary, she told herself. Perfectly natural. Certainly, there was nothing about an empty house like this to frighten anybody. And now she could turn on the light here in the upstairs hall. It had been papered in green stripes, and if *that* didn't frighten her, then nothing could. Ghastly!

She had her choice of three doors to enter

here. The first led to the bathroom. Lila had never seen such a place except in a museum — no, she corrected herself, they don't have bathroom exhibits in museums. But they should have had this one. An upright bathtub on legs; open pipes under the washstand and toilet seat; and dangling from the high ceiling next to the toilet, a metal pull-chain. There was a small mirror, flawed and flecked, over the washbowl, but no medicine cabinet behind it. Here was the linen closet, stacked with towels and bedding. She rummaged through the shelves hastily; their contents told her nothing except that Bates probably had his laundry sent out. The sheets were perfectly ironed, neatly folded.

Lila chose the second door, switched on the light. Another weak and naked overhead bulb, but its illumination was sufficient to reveal the room for what it was. Bates's bedroom — singularly small, singularly cramped, with a low cot more suitable for a little boy than a grown man. Probably he'd always slept here, even since he was a child. The bed itself was rumpled and showed signs of recent occupancy. There was a bureau over in the corner, next to the closet — one of those antique horrors with a dark oak finish and corroded drawer-pulls. She had no compunctions about searching the drawers.

The top one contained neckties and handkerchiefs, most of them soiled. The neckties were wide and old-fashioned. She found a tie clasp in a box from which it had apparently never been removed, and two sets of cuff links. The second drawer contained shirts, the third held socks and underwear. The bottom drawer was filled with white, shapeless garments which she finally — and almost incredulously — indentified as night-gowns. Maybe he wore a bedcap, too. Really, this whole house belonged in a museum!

It was odd that there were no personal mementos, though; no papers, no photographs. But then, perhaps he kept them down at the motel, in his desk there. Yes, that was very likely.

Lila turned her attention to the pictures on the walls. There were two of them. The first showed a small boy sitting on a pony, and the second showed the same child standing in front of a rural schoolhouse with five other children, all girls. It took Lila several moments before she identified the youngster as Norman Bates. He had been quite thin as a child.

Nothing remained, now, except the closet and the two large bookshelves in the corner. She disposed of the closet quickly; it contained two suits on hangers, a jacket, an overcoat, a pair of soiled and paint-spotted trousers. There was nothing in any of the pockets of these garments. Two pairs of shoes and a pair of bedroom slippers on the floor completed the inventory.

The bookshelves now.

Here Lila found herself pausing, puzzling, then peering in perplexity at the incongruous contents of Norman Bates's library. *A New Model of the Universe, The Extension of Consciousness, The Witch-Cult in Western Europe, Dimension and Being*. These were not the books of a small boy, and they were equally out of place in the home of a rural motel proprietor. She scanned the shelves rapidly. Abnormal psychology, occultism, theosophy. Translations of *Là Bas, Justine*. And here, on the bottom shelf, a non-descript assortment of untitled volumes, poorly bound. Lila pulled one out at random and opened it. The illustration that leaped out at her was almost pathologically pornographic.

She replaced the volume hastily and stood up. As she did so, the initial shock of revulsion ebbed away, giving place to a second, stronger reaction. There *was* something here, there must be. What she could not read in Norman Bates's dull, fat, commonplace face was all too vividly revealed here in his library.

Frowning, she retreated to the hall. The rain clattered harshly on the roof and thunder boomed as she opened the dark, paneled door leading to the third room. For a moment she stood staring into the dimness, inhaling a musty, mingled odor of stale perfume and — what?

She pressed the light switch at the side of the doorway, then gasped.

This was the front bedroom, no doubt of it. And the Sheriff had said something about how Bates had kept it unchanged since his mother's death. But Lila wasn't quite prepared for the actuality.

Lila wasn't quite prepared to step bodily into another era. And yet she found herself there, back in the world as it had been long before she was born.

For the décor of this room had been outmoded many years before Bates's mother died. It was a room such as she thought had not existed for the past fifty years; a room that belonged in a world of gilt ormolu clocks, Dresden figurines, sachet-scented pincushions, turkey-red carpet, tasseled draperies, frescoed vanity tops and four-poster beds; a room of rockers, china cats, of hand-embroidered bedspreads and over-stuffed chairs covered with antimacassars.

And it was still alive.

That was what gave Lila the feeling of dislocation in space and time. Downstairs were remnants of the past ravaged by decay, and upstairs all was shabbiness and neglect. But this room was composed, consistent, coherent; a vital, functioning entity complete unto itself. It was spotlessly clean, immaculately free of dust and perfectly ordered. And yet, aside from the musty odor, there was no feeling of being in a showplace or a museum. The room *did* seem alive, as does any room that is lived in for a long time. Furnished more than fifty years ago, untenanted and untouched since the death of its occupant twenty years ago, it was still the room of a living person. A room where, just yesterday, a woman had sat and peered out of the window —

There are no ghosts, Lila told herself, then frowned again at the realization that it had been necessary to make the denial. And yet, here in this room, she could feel a living presence.

She turned to the closet. Coats and dresses still hung in a neat row, though some of the garments were sagging and wrinkled through long lack of pressing. Here were the short skirts of a quarter of a century ago; up on the shelf the ornate hats, the head-scarves, several shawls such as an older woman might wear in a rural community. At the rear of the closet was a deep, empty recess which might have been meant for the storage of luggage. And nothing more.

Lila started over to examine the dresser and vanity, then halted beside the bed. The hand-embroidered bedspread was very lovely; she put out a hand to feel the texture, then drew it back hastily.

The bedspread was tucked in tightly at the bottom and hung perfectly over the sides. But the top was out of line. It had been tucked in, yes, but quickly, carelessly, so that an inch of the double pillow showed; the way a spread is tucked in when a bed has been made in a hurry —

She ripped the spread down, pulled back the covers. The sheets were a smudgy gray and covered with little brown flecks. But the bed itself, and the pillow above it, bore the faint yet unmistakable indentation made by a recent occupant. She could almost trace the outline of the body by the way the undersheet sagged, and there was a deep depression in the center of the pillow where the brown flecks were thickest.

There are no ghosts, Lila told herself again. This room has been used. Bates didn't sleep here — his own bed offered sufficient evidence of that. But somebody had been sleeping, somebody had been staring out of the window. *And if it had been Mary, where was she now?*

She could ransack the rest of the room, go through the drawers, search downstairs. But that wasn't important at the moment. There was something else she had to do first, if she could only remember. *Where was Mary, now?*

Then she knew.

What was it Sheriff Chambers had said? That he found Norman Bates down in the woods behind the house, gathering firewood?

Firewood for the furnace. Yes, that was it. *The furnace in the basement —*

Lila turned and fled down the stairs. The front door was open and the wind howled in. The front door was open, because she'd used the skeleton key, and now she knew why the term bothered her, it was because of the *skeleton* of course, and she knew why she had been so angry, too, ever since finding the earring. She had been angry because she was afraid, and the anger helped to hide the fear. The fear of what had happened to Mary, what she *knew* had happened to Mary, down in the cellar. It was because of Mary that she was afraid, not for herself. He had kept her here all week, maybe he'd tortured her, maybe he'd done to her what that man was doing in that filthy book, he'd tortured her until he found out about the money, and then —

The cellar. She had to find the cellar.

Lila groped her way along the downstairs hall, into the kitchen. She found the light, then gasped as the tiny furry creature crouched on the shelf before her, ready to spring. But it was only a stuffed squirrel, its button eyes idiotically alive in the reflection of the overhead light.

The basement stairs were just ahead. She fumbled at the wall until her hand brushed over another switch. The light went on below, just a faint and faltering glow in the darkened depths. Thunder growled in counterpoint to the clatter of her heels.

The bare bulb dangled from a cord directly in front of the furnace. It was a big furnace, with a heavy iron door. Lila stood there, staring at it. She was trembling now, she admitted that to herself; she could admit everything now. She'd been a fool to come here alone, a fool to do what she had done, a fool to do what she was doing now. But she had to do it, because of Mary. She had to open the furnace door and see what she knew would be inside. *God, what if the fire was still going? What if —*

But the door was cold. And there was no

heat from the furnace, no heat from within the dark, utterly empty recess behind the door. She stooped, peering, without even attempting to use the coal-poker. No ashes, no smell of burning, nothing at all. Unless it had been recently cleaned, the furnace hadn't been used since last spring.

Lila turned away. She saw the old-fashioned laundry tubs, and the table and chair beyond them, next to the wall. There were bottles on the table, and carpentry tools, plus an assortment of knives and needles. Some of the knives were oddly curved, and several of the needles were attached to syringes. Behind them rose a clutter of wooden blocks, heavy wire, and large shapeless blobs of a white substance she could not immediately identify. One of the bigger fragments looked something like the cast she had worn as a child, that time she'd broken her leg. Lila approached the table, gazing at the knives in puzzled concentration.

Then she heard the sound.

At first she thought it was thunder, but then came the creaking from overhead, and she knew.

Somebody had come into the house. Somebody was tiptoeing along the hall. Was it Sam? Had he come to find her? But then why didn't he call her name?

And why did he close the cellar door?

The cellar door *had* closed, just now. She could hear the sharp click of the lock, and the footsteps moving away, back along the hall. The intruder must be going upstairs to the second floor.

She was locked in the cellar. And there was no way out. No way out, nowhere to hide. The whole basement was visible to anyone descending the cellar stairs. And somebody would be coming down those stairs soon. She knew it now.

If she could only keep herself concealed for a moment, then whoever came after her would have to descend all the way into the basement. And she'd have a chance to run for the stairs, then.

The best place would be under the stairway itself. If she could cover up with some old papers or some rags —

Then Lila saw the blanket pinned to the far wall. It was a big Indian blanket, ragged and old. She tugged at it, and the rotted cloth ripped free of the nails which held it in place. It came off the wall, off the door.

The door. The blanket had concealed it completely, but there must be another room here, probably an old-fashioned fruit cellar. That would be the ideal place to hide and wait.

And she wouldn't have to wait much longer. Because now she could hear the faint, faraway footsteps coming down the hall again, moving along into the kitchen.

Lila opened the door of the fruit cellar.

It was then that she screamed.

She screamed when she saw the old woman lying there, the gaunt, gray-haired old woman whose brown, wrinkled face grinned up at her in an obscene greeting.

'Mrs. Bates!' Lila gasped.

'Yes.'

But the voice wasn't coming from those sunken, leathery jaws. It came from behind her, from the top of the cellar stairs, where the figure stood.

Lila turned to stare at the fat, shapeless figure, half-concealed by the tight dress which had been pulled down incongruously to cover the garments beneath. She stared up at the shrouding shawl, and at the white, painted, simpering face beneath it. She stared at the garishly reddened lips, watched them part in a convulsive grimace.

'I am Norma Bates,' said the high, shrill voice. And then there was the hand coming out, the hand that held the knife, and the feet were mincing down the stairs, and other feet were running, and Lila screamed again as Sam came down the stairs and the knife came up, quick as death. Sam grasped and twisted the hand that held it, twisted it from behind until the knife clattered to the floor.

Lila closed her mouth, but the scream continued. It was the insane scream of a hysterical woman, and it came from the throat of Norman Bates.

16

It took almost a week to reclaim the cars and the bodies from the swamp. The county highway crew had to come in with a dredger and hoists, but in the end the job was done. They found the money, too, right there in the glove compartment. Funny thing, it didn't even have a speck of mud on it, not a speck.

Somewhere along about the time they finished with the swamp, the men who knocked over the bank at Fulton were captured down in Oklahoma. But the story rated less than half a column in the Fairvale *Weekly Herald*. Almost the entire front page was given over to the Bates case. AP and UP picked it up right away, and there was quite a bit about it on television. Some of the write-ups compared it to the Gein affair up north, a few years back. They worked up a sweat over the 'house of horror' and tried their damnedest to make out that Norman Bates had been murdering motel visitors for years. They called for a complete investigation of every missing person case in the entire area for the past two decades, and urged that the entire swamp be drained to see if it would yield more bodies.

But then, of course, the newspaper writers didn't have to foot the bill for such a project.

Sheriff Chambers gave out a number of interviews, several of which were actually printed in full — two of them with photographs. He promised a full investigation of all aspects of the case. The local district attorney called for a speedy trial (primary election was coming in October) and did nothing to directly contradict the written and oral rumors which were circulating in which Norman Bates was portrayed as guilty of cannibalism, Satanism, incest, and necrophilia.

Actually, of course, he had never even talked to Bates, who was now temporarily confined for observation at the State Hospital.

Neither had the rumor-mongers, but that didn't stop them. Long before the week was out, it was beginning to appear that virtually the entire population of Fairvale, to say nothing of the entire county area south of there, had been personally and intimately acquainted with Norman Bates. Some of them had 'gone to school with him when he was a boy' and even then they had all 'noticed something funny about the way he acted.' Quite a few had 'seen him around that motel of his,' and they too attested to the fact that they'd always 'suspected' him. There were those who remembered his mother and Joe Considine, and they tried to establish how they 'knew something was wrong when those two were supposed to have committed suicide that way,' but of course the gruesome tidbits of twenty years ago seemed stale indeed as compared to more recent revelations.

The motel, of course, was closed — which seemed a pity, in a way, because there was no end to the number of morbid curiosity-lovers who sought it out. Quite conceivably, a goodly percentage would have been eager to rent rooms, and a slight raise in rates would compensate for the loss of the towels which undoubtedly would have been filched as souvenirs of the gala occasion. But State Highway Patrol troopers guarded the motel and the property behind it.

Even Bob Summerfield was able to report a noticeable increase of business at the hardware store. Everybody wanted to talk to Sam, naturally, but he spent part of the following week in Fort Worth with Lila, then took a run up to the State Hospital where three psychiatrists were examining Norman Bates.

It wasn't until almost ten days later, however, that he was finally able to get a definite statement from Dr. Nicholas Steiner, who was officially in charge of the medical observation.

Sam reported the results of his interview to Lila, at the hotel, when she came in from Fort Worth the following weekend. He was noticeably reticent at first, but she insisted on the full details.

'We'll probably never know everything that happened,' Sam told her, 'and as for the reasons, Dr. Steiner told me himself that it was mostly a matter of making an educated guess. They kept Bates under heavy sedation at first, and even after he came out of it, nobody could get him to really talk very much. Steiner says he got closer to Bates than anyone else, but in the last few days he appears to be in a very confused state. A lot of the things he said, about fugue and cathexis and trauma, are way over my head.

'But as near as he can make out, this all started way back in Bates's childhood, long before his mother's death. He and his mother were very close, of course, and apparently she dominated him. Whether there was ever anything more to their relationship, Dr. Steiner doesn't know. But he does suspect that Norman was a secret transvestite long before Mrs. Bates died. You know what a transvestite is, don't you?'

Lila nodded. 'A person who dresses in the clothing of the opposite sex, isn't that it?'

'Well, the way Steiner explained it, there's a lot more to it than that. Transvestites aren't necessarily homosexual, but they identify themselves strongly with members of the other sex. In a way, Norman wanted to be like his mother, and in a way he wanted his mother to become a part of himself.'

Sam lit a cigarette. 'I'm going to skip the data about his school years, and his rejection by the army. But it was after that, when he was around nineteen, that his mother must have decided Norman wasn't ever going out into the world on his own. Maybe she deliberately prevented him from growing up; we'll never actually know just how much she was responsible for what he became. It was probably then that he began to develop his interest in occultism, things like that. And it was then that this Joe Considine came into the picture.

'Steiner couldn't get Norman to say very much about Joe Considine — even today, more than twenty years later, his hatred is so great he can't talk about the man without flying into a rage. But Steiner talked to the Sheriff and dug up all the old newspaper stories, and he has a pretty fair idea of what really happened.

'Considine was a man in his early forties; when he met Mrs. Bates she was thirty-nine. I guess she wasn't much to look at, on the skinny side and prematurely gray, but ever since her husband had run off and left her she had owned quite a bit of farm property he'd put in her own name. It had brought in a good income during all these years, and even though she paid out a fair amount to the couple who worked it for her, she was well off. Considine began to court her. It wasn't too easy — I gather Mrs. Bates hated men ever since her husband deserted her and the baby, and this is one of the reasons why she treated Norman the way she did, according to Dr. Steiner. But I was telling you about Considine. He finally got her to come around and agree to a marriage. He'd brought up this idea of selling the farm and using the money to build a motel — the old highway ran right alongside the place in those days, and there was a lot of business to be had.

'Apparently Norman had no objections to the motel idea. The plan went through without a hitch, and for the first three months he and his mother ran the new place together. It was then, and only then, that his mother told him that she and Considine were going to be married.'

'And that sent him off?' Lila asked.

Sam ground out his cigarette in the ash tray. It was a good excuse for him to turn away as he answered. 'Not exactly, according to what Dr. Steiner found out. It seems the announcement was made under rather embarrassing circumstances, after Norman had walked in on his mother and Considine together in the upstairs bedroom. Whether the full effect of the shock was experienced immediately or whether it took quite a while for the reaction to set in, we don't know. But we do know what happened as a result. Norman poisoned his mother and Considine with strychnine. He used some kind of rat poison, served it to them with their coffee. I guess he waited until they had some sort of private celebration together; anyway there was a big dinner on the table, and the coffee was laced with brandy. It must have helped to kill the taste.'

'Horrible!' Lila shuddered.

'From all I hear, it *was*. The way I understand it, strychnine poisoning brings on convulsions, but not unconsciousness. The victims usually die from asphyxiation, when the chest muscles stiffen. Norman must have watched it all. And it was too much to bear.

'It was when he was writing the suicide note that Dr. Steiner thinks it happened. He had planned the note, of course, and knew how to imitate his mother's handwriting perfectly. He'd even figured out a reason — something about a pregnancy, and Considine being unable to marry because he had a wife and family living out on the West Coast, where he'd lived under another name. Dr. Steiner says the wording of the note itself would be enough to tip off anyone that something was wrong. But nobody noticed, any more than they noticed what really happened to Norman after he finished the note and phoned the Sheriff to come out.

'They knew, at the time, that he was hysterical from shock and excitement. What they didn't know is that while writing the note, he'd changed. Apparently, now that it was all over, he couldn't stand the loss of his mother. He wanted her back. As he wrote the note in her handwriting, addressed to himself, he literally *changed his mind*. And Norman, or a part of him, *became* his mother.

'Dr. Steiner says these cases are more frequent than you'd think, particularly when the personality is already unstable, as Norman's was. And the grief set him off. His reaction was so severe, nobody even thought to question the suicide pact. Both Considine and his mother were in their graves long before Norman was discharged from the hospital.'

'And that's when he dug her up?' Lila frowned.

'Apparently he did so, within a few months at most. He had this taxidermy hobby, and knew what he'd have to do.'

'But I don't understand. If he thought he *was* his mother, then — '

'It isn't quite that simple. According to Steiner, Bates was now a multiple personality with at least three facets. There was *Norman*, the little boy who needed his mother and hated anything or anyone who came between him and her. Then, *Norma*, the mother, who could not be allowed to die. The third aspect might be called *Normal* — the adult Norman Bates, who had to go through the daily routine of living, and conceal the existence of the other personalities from the world. Of course, the three weren't entirely distinct entities, and each contained elements of the other. Dr. Steiner called it an 'unholy trinity.'

'But the adult Norman Bates kept control well enough so that he was discharged from the hospital. He went back to run the motel, and it was then that he felt the strain. What weighed on him most, as an adult personality, was the guilty knowledge of his mother's death. Preserving her room was not enough. He wanted to preserve her, too; preserve her physically, so that the illusion of her living

219

presence would suppress the guilt feelings.

'So he brought her back, actually brought her back from the grave and gave her a new life. He put her to bed at night, dressed her and took her down into the house by day. Naturally, he concealed all this from outsiders and he did it well. Arbogast must have seen the figure placed in the upstairs window, but there's no proof that anyone else did, in all those years.'

'Then the horror wasn't in the house,' Lila murmured. 'It was in his head.'

'Steiner says the relationship was like that of a ventriloquist and his dummy. Mother and *little* Norman must have carried on regular conversations. And the adult Norman Bates probably rationalized the situation. He was able to pretend sanity, but who knows how much he really knew? He was interested in occultism and metaphysics. He probably believed in spiritualism every bit as much as he believed in the preservative powers of taxidermy. Besides, he couldn't reject or destroy these other parts of his personality without rejecting and destroying himself. He was leading three lives at once.

'And the point is, he was getting away with it, until — '

Sam hesitated, but Lila finished the sentence for him. 'Until Mary came along.

And something happened, and he killed her.'

'Mother killed her,' Sam said. '*Norma* killed your sister. There's no way of finding out the actual situation, but Dr. Steiner is sure that whenever a crisis arose, *Norma* became the dominant personality. Bates would start drinking, then black out while *she* took over. During the blackouts, of course, he'd dress up in her clothing. Afterward he'd hide her image away, because in his mind she was the real murderer and had to be protected.'

'Then Steiner is quite sure he's insane?'

'Psychotic — that's the word he used. Yes, I'm afraid so. He's going to recommend that Bates be placed in the State Hospital, probably for life.'

'Then there won't be any trial?'

'That's what I came here to tell you. No, there won't be any trial.' Sam sighed heavily. 'I'm sorry. I suppose the way you feel — '

'I'm glad,' Lila said slowly. 'It's better this way. Funny, how differently things work out in real life. None of us really suspected the truth, we just blundered along until we did the right things for the wrong reasons. And right now, I can't even hate Bates for what he did. He must have suffered more than any of us. In a way I can almost understand. We're all not quite as sane as we pretend to be.'

Sam rose, and she walked him to the door. 'Anyway, it's over, and I'm going to try to forget it. Just forget everything that happened.'

'Everything?' Sam murmured. He didn't look at her.

'Well, *almost* everything.' She didn't look at him.

And that was the end of it.

Or *almost* the end.

17

The real end came quietly.

It came in the small, barred room where the voices had muttered and mingled for so long a time — the man's voice, the woman's voice, the child's.

The voices had exploded when triggered into fission, but now, almost miraculously, a fusion took place.

So that there was only one voice. And that was right, because there was only one person in the room. There always *had* been one person, and *only* one.

She knew it now.

She knew it, and she was glad.

It was so much better to be this way; to be fully and completely aware of one's self as one *really* was. To be serenely strong, serenely confident, serenely secure.

She could look back upon the past as though it were all a bad dream, and that's just what it had been: a bad dream, peopled with illusions.

There had been a bad boy in the bad dream, a bad boy who had killed her lover and tried to poison her. Somewhere in the dream was the strangling and the wheezing and the clawing at the throat and the faces that turned blue. Somewhere in the dream was the graveyard at night and the digging and the panting and the splintering of the coffin lid, and then the moment of discovery, the moment of staring at what lay within. But what lay within wasn't really dead. Not any more. The bad boy was dead, instead, and that was as it should be.

There had been a bad man in the bad dream, too, and he was also a murderer. He had peeked through the wall and he drank, and he read filthy books and believed in all sorts of crazy nonsense. But worst of all, he was responsible for the deaths of two innocent people — a young girl with beautiful breasts and a man who wore a gray Stetson hat. She knew all about it, of course, and that's why she could remember the details. Because she had been there at the time, watching. But all she did was watch.

The bad man had really committed the murders and then he tried to blame it on her.

Mother killed them. That's what he said, but it was a lie.

How could she kill them when she was only watching, when she couldn't even move because she had to pretend to be a stuffed figure, a harmless stuffed figure that couldn't hurt or be hurt but merely exists forever?

She knew that nobody would believe the bad man, and he was dead now, too. The bad man and the bad boy were both dead, or else they were just part of the dream. And the dream had gone away now for good.

She was the only one left, and she was real.

To be the only one, and to know that you are real — that's sanity, isn't it?

But just to be on the safe side, maybe it was best to keep pretending that one was a stuffed figure. Not to move. Never to move. Just to sit here in the tiny room, forever and ever.

If she sat there without moving, they wouldn't punish her.

If she sat here without moving, they'd know that she was sane, sane, sane.

She sat there for quite a long time, and then a fly came buzzing through the bars.

It lighted right on her hand.

If she wanted to, she could reach out and swat the fly.

But she didn't swat it.

She didn't swat it, and she hoped they were watching, because that *proved* what sort of a person she really was.

Why, she wouldn't even harm a fly . . .

We do hope that you have enjoyed reading this large print book.

Did you know that all of our titles are available for purchase?

We publish a wide range of high quality large print books including:
Romances, Mysteries, Classics
General Fiction
Non Fiction and Westerns

Special interest titles available in large print are:
The Little Oxford Dictionary
Music Book
Song Book
Hymn Book
Service Book

Also available from us courtesy of Oxford University Press:
Young Readers' Dictionary
(large print edition)
Young Readers' Thesaurus
(large print edition)

For further information or a free brochure, please contact us at:
Ulverscroft Large Print Books Ltd.,
The Green, Bradgate Road, Anstey,
Leicester, LE7 7FU, England.
Tel: (00 44) 0116 236 4325
Fax: (00 44) 0116 234 0205

THE SACRIFICE

Mike Uden

When private eye Pamela Andrews and her daughter, Anna, are chosen to investigate a high-profile case concerning the whereabouts of a missing girl, they wonder why. They're hardly household names and no one really expects them to succeed. Then the penny drops — they've just been cast as headline-grabbing eye-candy. With no help from the police and nothing much to work on, it soon becomes a daunting mission. Hunting down an abductor is one thing. Becoming the next victim is quite another . . .

THE ONE A MONTH MAN

Michael Litchfield

Thirty years ago, Oxford was a city of fear for female students, terrorized by a killer dubbed 'The One-A-Month Man' due to the ritualistic regularity of his crimes. Advances in DNA profiling since the time of the murders has identified Richard Pope, son of a US senator and now a frontline CIA operative, as the killer — and survivor Tina Marlowe finds herself in danger once more ... The bad but brilliant detective Mike Lorenzo, exiled from Scotland Yard, is assigned to trace Tina before she is tracked down by her lethal enemy — just the challenge he needs to redeem himself ...

AN INVISIBLE MURDER

Joyce Cato

When travelling cook Jenny Starling starts her new job at Avonsleigh Castle, she is thrilled. She envisions nothing more arduous than days spent preparing her beloved recipes. But when a fabulous bejewelled dagger, one of the castle's many art treasures, is used to murder a member of staff, the Lady of the House insists that Jenny help the police with their enquiries. But how was it done? The murder was committed in front of several impeccable witnesses, none of whom saw a thing. It seems the reluctant sleuth must once again discover the identity of the killer in their midst . . .

THE DOLL PRINCESS

Tom Benn

Manchester, July 1996, the month after the IRA bomb. The *Evening News* reports two murders. On the front page is a photograph of an heiress to an oil fortune, her body discovered in the basement of a block of flats . . . Buried in the later pages there's a fifty-word piece on the murder of a young prostitute. For Bane, it's the latter that hits hardest. Determined to find out what happened to his childhood sweetheart, it soon becomes clear that the two stories belong on the same page, as Bane immerses himself in a world of drugs, gun arsenals, human trafficking and a Manchester in decay . . .

SLEEPING DOGS

Fay Cunningham

Gina Cross is a forensic artist for the police. She teams up with Adam Shaw, an investigative journalist, to find Nathan Fox, a school caretaker, involved in the mystery of a child's death twenty years ago. Fox had found something that incriminated three of the students, but then he'd disappeared. The students are now grown up: one is a renowned plastic surgeon, one a politician and the third is a lawyer. But now Fox is back, and no one is safe — and she's not the only one hunting Fox. When Gina's friend is kidnapped and held hostage, anything, including murder, is on the cards.

OUT OF THE NIGHT

Dan Latus

One headless body, on the beach near Frank Doy's home on the Cleveland coast, was regrettable, two more were disturbing. But when an uncommunicative woman arrives at his house in the dead of night, only to disappear again, Doy is involved in something worrying. His search for her uncovers a mysterious man with a private art collection and some Russian emigres. Led deeper into the strange events occurring in Port Holland and nearby Meridion House, Frank tries to unearth the secrets surrounding him and save the life of his desperate female visitor . . .